WILD FATED

SHADOW PACK LEGENDS
BOOK THREE

LUNA M. ROSE

CHAPTER

ONE

LANA

The first light of morning filtered through the grimy curtains. Just enough to illuminate the peeling wallpaper and worn carpet. Delightful.

I stretched out my legs under the thin, scratchy blanket, which did little to ward off the morning chill seeping through the cracks in the window. The bathroom light flickered like it was trying to decide whether it wanted to live or die, throwing erratic shadows across the wall. This place looked like it hadn't been cleaned since the eighties, and I was sure as hell that was the last time the sheets had been washed.

I glanced over at Kael and Callista, both still sleeping on their lumpy queen mattress. Callista cuddled up to him, and I was mildly jealous of her built-in heater. Kael lay on his back, his arm draped over his eyes, his chest rising and falling in a

1

slow, measured rhythm. I was happy for them, but that picture of domestic bliss was a little bit disgusting.

I sat up, my muscles protesting, and the weight of the dagger pressed against my side. I pulled it out from beneath my coat, its hilt warm against my palm. The blade hummed against my skin like a living thing, and I ran my thumb over the intricate engravings.

It was strange, this connection I felt to it. Ever since I'd drawn it across my palm and let my blood seep into its metal, it had been with me. A constant presence. A silent companion. It didn't speak to me, but it didn't need to.

You already have a companion, my wolf growled.

A piece of metal isn't going to replace you, I shot back. I was equal parts terrified and intrigued by the things I felt happening in my body. To my wolf and my magic. And then there was the guilt and the grief.

Rowan had given me the go-ahead to leave our new Kootenay pack, but we'd barely blended Kitimat and Black Lake. This damn dagger had been the cause of a revolution, not only in our packs but all the packs in British Columbia. As the third to Rowan, my alpha, I'd been a leader in Black Lake. At least in my absence, Callista's brother Blake was there to step in.

I still didn't know if my school had found a replacement teacher for me. I'd left them a hurried message about my last-minute change of plans and received an email acknowledgment on Monday morning. They weren't happy with me, and I didn't blame them. I didn't know how long I was going to be gone, but I doubted I was going to find the rest of the relics and save the world in a week and a half. Which meant I was letting my school down, too.

Students didn't return until September. There was still a chance I could go back. But it wasn't looking good.

I slid the dagger back into place at my hip and stood to use the bathroom.

"Morning," Callie groaned from behind me.

I turned. "Hey."

"Ready to get on the road?"

I grinned. "More ready than you are."

Callista smirked and nudged Kael in the ribs. He grunted, and I stepped outside to give them some privacy.

Once we were all in the truck, I insisted we stop at a gas station. The only option for sustenance this far north. They could starve themselves if they wanted to, but I was done with it. We pulled into a lot surrounded by flickering neon signs and dingy storefronts. The store was half-empty, and the cashier barely looked up as we grabbed our breakfast burritos from the hot food case.

"These look like a culinary masterpiece," Callista muttered, picking up a burrito that oozed grease onto the wax paper.

I shrugged. "They can't be worse than the gas station sushi I had last month." She made a face, and I smirked. "Don't worry, I didn't die. Yet."

Kael didn't say a word, just grabbed a couple burritos for himself, curled them into the crook of his arm, then glanced at Callie and grabbed an extra. When we got back to the car, he handed it to her. "You need to eat more."

Callista rolled her eyes but took it. "For the last time, you are not my mother."

Kael just grunted and handed her napkins and a bottle of water.

I rolled my eyes. Those two were completely twitter pated. I hadn't known Kael for long, but he'd come a long way from trying to stab her in a tent. All of it was weird. Endearing, but weird.

I still don't trust him. My wolf sat back on her haunches. I rolled my eyes internally. She didn't trust anyone, so that wasn't anything new. After years, she'd finally stopped complaining about Rowan, so Kael didn't have any hope for the foreseeable future.

We sat in Kael's truck parked on the edge of the lot, the morning sun climbing higher in the sky. My burrito tasted faintly of sausage and eggs with a hint of regret.

"We should get there by two," Kael said.

"Then wait for nightfall?" Callista asked.

He shook his head. "It won't give us any advantage. We can park at a pull-out near the old mill. Then we'll shift and run the rest of the way. I'll scout things out."

I didn't argue with him. Normally, I would've made a bigger deal about me taking the lead, but he'd been there before. Possibly more than once. I still wasn't completely clear on how long he'd been with the alphas before he came to find Callista. It didn't matter now. He'd more than proven himself trustworthy.

The scenery outside the car window flicked past like a montage in an indie film as we drove—thick forests bleeding into barren fields. We drove past crumbling industrial buildings, their graffiti-covered walls standing as monuments to a forgotten era. The highways and backroads stretched out like veins, empty and desolate. The only signs of life were the occasional dilapidated farmhouses and rusted-out cars abandoned on the side of the road.

Kael's jaw was tight as he drove. "You shouldn't have brought the dagger." He glanced over at me, then back out the windshield.

"I couldn't leave it."

Kael tapped his fingers on the wheel. "They'll know you have it. You'll have to stay far—"

Hell, no, my wolf growled. I agreed wholeheartedly. "I'm not letting you go in there without me."

Kael exhaled sharply and glanced down at Callista next to him on the bench. I knew what he was thinking. Yes, he wanted me to be safe. But he was infinitely more concerned with his mate. I couldn't blame him. But I wasn't going to stay back and watch, either.

"Let's see what we're working with. Then we can make decisions about who's going where." Callista plugged the cord dangling from the dash into her phone and started a playlist. We listened to music for the next couple of hours until Kael pulled off the main road. After a few minutes of jostling over gravel, he drove the truck into the trees.

Kael threw the truck into park, cutting the engine. The sudden quiet wrapped around us. He and Callista slid out of the truck first, heading to the back to grab their packs, and I followed, my boots sinking into the soft mulch. The forest loomed around us, thick and shadowed even though it was the middle of the afternoon.

Kael popped open the truck bed, and we pulled out our packs that held extra clothes, water bottles, food, and emergency supplies we might need if things went south. I double-checked my pack, then slid the dagger in with the rest of my things.

Callista slung her pack over one shoulder and gave me a quick look. "You good?"

I nodded, already pulling off my jacket. Shifting wasn't something I liked to do in front of others—something about being that vulnerable, even with people I trusted, made me twitchy. "I'll meet you in a minute."

Kael arched a brow but didn't comment. He and Callista exchanged a glance, then disappeared into the woods together. I heard the soft rustle of clothes being stripped off behind the trees, followed by the low growls and stretching sounds of two wolves taking form. I stayed by the truck, peeling off my layers quickly and stuffing them into my pack. The cold air bit at my skin as I shifted, fur replacing skin in a smooth ripple of change. My wolf settled beneath my bones, itching to run, to find what waited for us at the building ahead.

Once I was in wolf form, I could feel Callista through the pack bond, a warm, steady hum at the back of my mind.

Ready? Her voice came through the link. She was already moving.

Right behind you, I answered. Callista and I could communicate freely through the pack bond, even though we were miles from the heart of the Kootenay pack's territory. But Kael? He wasn't officially one of us yet. I couldn't hear him directly. Not like she could as his mate. For the time being, Callista was our mediator.

The three of us took off through the forest, weaving between trees and leaping over undergrowth. Callista and Kael moved as one, their wolves in perfect sync. It was strange, being part of a pack and yet not. I was looking for the Shadow Pack, to find a piece of myself that didn't have a place in Kootenay or anywhere else.

But it was at the expense of this.

Would I ever run with my pack again? I'd been Rowan's third, responsible for keeping order, for standing between the pack and anything that threatened it. That had been my job— to protect the humans in our territory and keep the dark things at bay. Enemies of shifters lurked on the edges of the world, and it was our job to keep them there, no matter the cost. It was simple. It made sense.

I'd worked next to Rowan and Jasper for years, and now? What would my role be if I wasn't in Black Lake or Kootenay anymore? What if I couldn't find the other relics?

We slowed as the forest thinned, and the outline of the building emerged through the trees, a dark silhouette against the dimming sky. Kael's wolf went rigid, ears pricked forward.

Callista's voice touched my mind again. *Let's scout the perimeter. See if there's anyone here.*

Kael let out a low growl in protest, circling Callista briefly. He didn't like splitting up from her—I could feel that loud and clear, even without hearing his thoughts directly. But she nudged him back with a flick of her tail, and I wished I could hear whatever words she sent his direction.

Reluctantly, Kael fell back beside me, his muscles coiled. Part of me hoped one of the alphas threatened Callista. I'd love to see how fast Kael ripped out their throat.

Together, we moved through the underbrush, working our way toward the building from different angles, each step careful and deliberate. We circled, searching for any sign of life, but found nothing.

No vehicles. No lights. No movement. Even the scents I picked up felt stale.

Anything? I pushed to Callista. All I got back was a low growl of frustration. When we met up back where we'd started, Kael didn't waste any time shifting back to human form. I turned and did the same, quickly pulling my clothes from the backpack.

After tying my boots, I stood and wove through the trees to the entrance.

Kael blocked my way. "We don't know what's inside."

"Isn't your friend inside? That's why we're here, right?" I snapped, then pursed my lips. I wasn't angry with Kael or Callista. I was just on edge.

Kael stepped back, giving me a look. We both knew I wasn't there for his friend. I was there because the alphas were ten steps ahead of us in searching for these relics. They'd already found the dagger. There was a good chance they had a lead on another one, and I needed to know what they knew.

"Give me a couple of minutes." Kael set down his pack, then stalked off before either of us could argue. He was learning. I had to give him that.

Callista watched him go, then started twisting her fingers together.

"He'll be fine," I murmured.

"They'll kill him if they find him."

I scoffed. "I doubt they trap like I do, and with you here, I think he'd cut through all three of them without blinking."

Callista gave a nervous laugh. "How are you holding up?"

I shrugged. "Fine. How's Blake?"

"He's good. Honestly, I think he likes feeling needed. He drifted in the days after Kitimat dissolved."

I understood that. Better than anyone at the moment.

Kael appeared next to us a few moments later, breathing hard. "I can't see any signs of life."

"Perfect. Then what are we waiting for?"

"Lana," Kael's voice was low, a warning.

I took a deep breath, forcing myself to meet his eyes. They were like storm clouds, dark and swirling with barely contained fury. "I know. I know it's stupid to rush in. But I can't just sit here. It's pulling me. I can't explain it, but I have to go in."

Kael stared at me for a moment longer, then exhaled slowly. He glanced at Callista, who gave a small nod. "Fine. But we go in together. And we stay together."

DESTIN

I lay curled in the corner of the cell, every part of my body aching, muscles stiff from the cold concrete floor beneath me. My wolf kept me alive, but just barely. Healing was slow without food or water, my strength slipping away by the hour. My ribs cut against my skin, and hunger gnawed at me, the kind that sat deep in my bones. More than just an empty stomach—it was weakness spreading like rot.

I'd tried to shift back to human form earlier, but my body rejected it, too exhausted to make the change. I was stuck like this, fur matted and caked with blood that I couldn't wash away. The wounds from the last beating still throbbed, sluggish and raw.

And yet, even through the pain, a small flicker of pride burned inside me. Kael hadn't come back with the dagger. That alone told me everything I needed to know. The northern alphas didn't own him, not completely. He didn't let them twist him the way they wanted, didn't bring back that cursed blade to hand over like a loyal dog. If they'd come after me for it, that meant Kael ran. That was good. Better to be hunted than leashed to them. Kael was worth more than that life, even if it had taken him years to figure it out. I just hoped he stayed smart enough to remain free.

But that thought twisted into a deeper ache. The wolves back in my territory. The rogues. The lost ones. The shifters the packs couldn't be bothered to protect. They depended on me, and every day I was stuck here was another day they were exposed to danger.

Packs had never done anything for wolves like me or the ones I watched over. If anything, they caused more harm than good. They'd thrown me away when I didn't fit their mold, exiled me because I wasn't what they wanted. Kael, too. The moment they saw his malformed arm, they cast him out like garbage without a second thought. I'd seen it too many times, and each incident only strengthened my resolve. Packs didn't care for us. We cared for each other. Full stop.

That's why I had to stay alive. The relics were the worst of it. Power in the hands of alphas, unchecked and unchallenged. If the northern alphas thought they could bend every wolf to their will with that dagger, they were fools. No one should wield that kind of power, not over wolves like me, not over anyone.

I breathed against the cold floor, trying to think through the haze of hunger. I needed a plan. I refused to die here, not like this—starving, dehydrated, abandoned in some gods-forsaken cell. The alphas were gone for the moment. Two days, maybe more, since I'd heard anything. No footsteps. No voices. No water sloshed through the grate.

Whatever game they were playing, they'd left without

finishing it. I just didn't know why. If I couldn't get out of this cell soon, I wouldn't need to worry about the relics or the alphas or anything else—I'd rot right here.

My claws scraped against stone. I needed to save my strength, but the wolf inside me was restless, ready to tear through anything just for the chance to live. I closed my eyes, breathing slowly through the pain, trying to make a plan with what little I had left. Maybe if I tried again to shift back to my human form, I could break something—dislocate a joint and slip free. Maybe not. Hell, maybe I'd just smash my wolf head against the bars until something gave. It wouldn't be the worst plan I'd come up with.

And then—footsteps. Faint, distant, but unmistakable. My ears pricked, my body tensing despite the weariness dragging me down. Someone was coming. I lifted my head slowly, every muscle in my body taut. It wasn't the heavy thud of the alphas nor the careless shuffle of a guard. These steps were different. Intentional. My breath came slower, quieter, as I stayed perfectly still.

If this was my chance, I wasn't going to waste it.

CHAPTER
THREE

LANA

I pushed open the door and stepped into dank stillness. The air smelled stale, like it had been trapped in a cellar for years. Strange since Kael had met with the northern alphas within the last few weeks.

My wolf stood at attention, her muscles coiled. *I don't like this.*

Yeah. Me, either.

Kael's tension was palpable, his eyes scanning the shadows that crept along the walls. He sensed it, too. The wrongness, the feeling that we were walking into something we weren't prepared for. We ventured deeper into the building, our footsteps echoing in the silence. It pressed in around us, suffocating. I gripped the dagger tighter. I didn't know if it should be used as a weapon, but I felt safer with it in my hands.

We moved silently through the dim hallways, the hair on

the back of my neck standing on end. Kael kept close to Callista, his gaze sharp and vigilant as he positioned himself just slightly in front of her.

We paused at the edge of the next corridor, Kael lifting his hand to signal us to stop. His nostrils flared. I crouched beside him as he scanned the hall ahead, his fingers brushing the wall. His wolf pressed so close to the surface, my wolf felt a little left out.

Callista rested a hand briefly on his back. Kael tilted his head toward her. "Something doesn't feel right. There should be movement. Guards. I don't like this."

Neither did I. The building was too quiet, too easy. No scents lingered. Kael, of all people, understood that magic since he had unexplainable abilities, but from the look on his face, he wasn't aware anyone else was capable of it besides him.

"Did they mask their scents?" I asked.

Kael shook his head. "I'm not sure. But I don't know how else they would've done it."

"Or why." Callista clenched her jaw as we crept forward.

When we reached the next corner, Kael signaled us to stop again, his eyes narrowing as he tilted his head, listening.

Nothing.

No sounds of guards patrolling, no movement beyond the walls. Just silence.

Satisfied—though not at ease—Kael motioned for us to continue. Callista stayed close to his side, the two of them moving in sync. His hand brushed hers briefly as if she needed the reassurance.

We turned the corner and stepped into a large room. Bookshelves lined the walls. Maps were spread over tables. I pressed against the wall, waiting for an alarm to sound or for wolves to spring from the corners.

But there was nothing. No guards. No alphas. Just us.

"We need to get out," Kael growled.

Not yet. My wolf willed me toward the maps, and I stalked forward obediently.

Callista tensed. "Lana, there's something wrong—"

"I'm aware," I snapped. But I wasn't going to give up this opportunity to see what the alphas had been researching.

"Why would they have left this out?" Kael looked like his wolf was going to tear out of him.

"It doesn't matter. I need to see—"

"If it was important, they would've taken it with them."

"Maybe they didn't have a choice." My brain spun with possibilities. Had something or someone threatened the alphas? Had they left when they realized Kael wasn't coming back?

I tore through the papers scattered across the desk, my fingers flipping through old notebooks and useless ledgers. What were they keeping track of, their grocery purchases? *On paper?*

There had to be something here about the relics, something we could use. Most of the books on the desk were about the old legends: the rise and fall of the Shadow Pack, the prophecies about the relics returning, and the supposed power locked inside each one. It was mind-boggling that in the course of a week, this information had become old hat.

Kael prowled behind me, his presence buzzing at the edge of my awareness. Tension rolled off him, the way he kept glancing toward the hallway. We had different priorities. Yes, Kael and Callista had committed to helping me unearth information on the rest of the relics, but until we figured out where Kael's friend Destin was, he wasn't going to be able to focus on that.

"Just go," I muttered. There still wasn't any sign of life in the building. If this was a trap by the northern alphas, wouldn't they have sprung it by now?

"I'm not leaving you here alone."

I shot him a look but knew it wouldn't change anything. He was on high alert for his mate. I was just caught in the cross-fire. I shoved his agitation aside and bent closer to the papers. I needed to make sense of all this. I had to.

After scanning the mess of papers and books faster than a high school literature assignment, I finally saw it. A tattered piece of paper was buried beneath a ledger, half hidden under ink-covered pages. I carefully pulled it free, the brittle edges flaking under my touch. My heart kicked up as I scanned the faded letters, the words barely visible. But there it was. A mention of another relic. A book.

I frowned, processing the words in front of me. Lava Forks. A sacred site. Deep in the mountains. Was that where the alphas thought it was hidden?

I held up the paper to Kael. "This is why they aren't here."

He took it from me, his brow furrowing as he read. "You think they found it."

I gestured at the empty room. "You said it yourself. They wouldn't have left this without a good reason." He handed the paper back, and I slipped it into my jacket pocket. This was the first real lead we had, though it raised more questions than it answered. "Do you know anything about Lava Forks?" I asked.

Kael shook his head. "We can get into that later."

Callista took his hand. There was no sound. No scent. I glanced down and scanned the desk one final time, my eyes snagging on a title that sat on the corner. Legends of the Shadow Pack. It was a storybook. One I'd seen before but couldn't quite place. I picked it up and shoved it in my bag.

"They may have taken your friend with them." I took a step

toward the door. I hoped they'd taken him with them. Otherwise . . .

Kael's expression hardened as he turned. We made our way back into the hallway, Kael taking the lead with Callista close behind. He pushed into the two other rooms on the main floor and found them empty, then took the stairs at the end of the hall.

The stairwell groaned under our weight as we descended, the light from the windows above struggling to reach the basement. The deeper we went, the colder and heavier the air became. Kael was a wall of tension ahead of me, his shoulders stiff. Even Callista looked like she might jump out of her skin at the tiniest sound. At least they didn't trust this place any more than I did.

As we reached the lower level, the scent of old blood hit me like a slap. It clung to the walls, thick and metallic. My wolf stirred uneasily, sensing the same thing I did. Kael stopped short before a rusted metal door, his jaw clenched tight. The hinges groaned as he pushed it open, revealing the dingy room beyond, and—

The sight inside stopped me cold. Bars. Reinforced walls. A massive black wolf was curled in the corner of a makeshift cell, its fur coated in layers of filth and blood. His ribs made impressions through his fur, and dark stains streaked the floor where he'd tried—and failed—to escape.

"Is that—" I started to ask, then snapped my mouth shut when a low growl rumbled from the wolf's throat, vibrating through the walls of the tiny cell.

I shuddered, my wolf baring her teeth. She knew that sound. This wolf was starving. Desperate. And dangerous.

Destin

Kael's scent hit me first—familiar but distant, like something from another life. My wolf stirred, a flicker of recognition buried beneath the exhaustion and rage. But it wasn't enough. The snarl slipped out before I could stop it, a low, guttural warning that rumbled through my chest. My jaws twitched, lips curling back over my teeth. He was too close. Too familiar. And right now, nothing familiar felt safe.

Kael took a slow step forward, his voice low and steady, like he was trying to coax a wounded animal. "It's me, Destin. You're safe now."

Safe. The word meant nothing. Safe was a lie people told to make you drop your guard, and the wolf in me knew better than to fall for it. My glowing eyes locked on him, wild and full of warning. I hated the way he crouched in front of the bars, calm and patient, like he still believed I was something that could be reasoned with.

My muscles screamed as I pushed against the cold concrete, trying to lift myself. My paws scrabbled against the floor, useless and weak, my body too starved to obey me. I barely got my head an inch off the ground before it dropped back down, a growl of frustration rumbling deep in my throat. Every inch of me should've been aching. But I felt nothing.

Kael crouched closer, his gaze steady as if daring me to snap. His hand moved slowly, careful not to spook me, fingers brushing the lock on the door.

"Easy, Destin," he murmured, keeping his voice soft. It grated against my ears—too kind, too steady. He was treating me like something fragile. I wasn't fragile. I was broken. There was a difference.

My wolf shifted restlessly inside me, torn between the instinct to lash out and the faint flicker of trust buried somewhere in my chest. *Kael wasn't the enemy.* The truth floated, slipping through my thoughts before I could grasp it.

And then I caught the scent. Kael wasn't the only shifter in the room. He'd brought another—his mate. I could smell their bond. And . . . there was one more. Her scent burned through me like whiskey. *Where was she?* I searched but couldn't see her.

He was hiding her from me. I couldn't trust what I was seeing. Kael wasn't alone. They could say all the words they wanted, but words meant nothing. They hadn't fed me, hadn't helped me heal, they'd left me here to rot, and my body was still paying the price for it. The growl in my chest deepened.

Kael ran a hand through his hair, frustration clear in the way his shoulders tightened. "Last time I saw him, he was already slipping," he muttered to the others. "More wolf than man. I don't know what the alphas did to him, but they might've pushed him over the edge."

I tried again to push myself from the floor, and when I dropped, the concrete bit into my jaw. Kael's voice kept coming, calm and patient. "We're going to help you, Destin. Just stay with me. Trust me." He made himself small—hand visible, shoulders relaxed—but it grated against my nerves.

Then the light changed, and *she* stepped into view. The second she-wolf. Her scent swirled through the bars in my cell. My eyes snapped to her, and something inside me stilled. It was like falling into cold water, a jolt that froze my thoughts mid-motion. My paws rooted to the stone floor, muscles locking as I stared. Everything around me blurred for a second, narrowing to just her.

She stepped forward, her gaze flickering between me and Kael, confusion mixed with unease. Kael watched me, his dark eyes boring into me, noting the change in my demeanor. "Don't even think about it," he hissed. His jaw clenched as he put out a hand to stop her from moving any closer to my cell.

The woman cleared her throat. "How do we get him out of there?"

"I'm not touching this door until he pulls himself together."

She glanced over her shoulder, and the other woman appeared. Kael's mate. *Kael had a mate.* That thought sent warmth flickering for a brief moment within me.

"He's not going to do anything. Look at him." The first woman glanced at me, then dropped her eyes to the floor. "He can't even lift his own weight."

Kael scoffed. "Yeah. Don't underestimate him."

Kael ran his hand over the door's edge, tracing the heavy bolts securing it in place. "It's reinforced. They weren't playing around." He glanced at his mate, who stood beside him, her brows furrowed. "We should check for keys."

The other woman in black—it wasn't only her hair, she

was clothed in it—nodded, already scanning the walls. I tracked her carefully, curiosity biting at the edges of my mind.

Kael's mate sifted through a metal box mounted on the wall, her fingers brushing over loose tools and random junk. She shook her head. "Nothing here."

The other woman crouched near the far wall, running her hands along a row of hooks and shelves cluttered with old equipment. "Got something." She held up a small ring of keys. They jingled softly, the sound echoing off the concrete walls.

Kael stepped toward her and took them. "Let's see if one of these damn things works." He tried the first key, sliding it into the lock. It turned halfway before jamming. He cursed under his breath and moved to the next. The woman in black stayed beside him, her sharp gaze darting between the lock and the hallway.

"No good," Kael muttered, tossing the keys aside with a frustrated growl. "We'll have to break it."

He grabbed a crowbar, wedging it into the frame. The metal groaned, giving slightly under the pressure. Kael grunted, but the lock didn't budge. The door fought back, stubborn as hell, and the grinding of metal on metal made my ears twitch. "This isn't going to work," Kael growled.

I stayed where I was, watching them through narrowed eyes. Then the woman in black stepped away, and a low whine left my muzzle without permission. Kael's nostrils flared.

"Umm, how about this?" The woman stalked across the room like she owned the place, her boots soft against the concrete. She stopped in the corner, crouched, and dragged out a heavy, portable hydraulic jack.

Kael's mate gave a skeptical snort. "What is that?"

The woman grinned, setting the jack down near the door. "This is a jack. I knew there was a reason I took shop." She adjusted the arms with ease, sliding the jack into place beneath the doorframe as if this were the most natural thing in the world.

Kael pulled his hand from his pocket. "I can—"

"I've got this." She flicked his hand away. "This little beast can lift a truck. A door's nothing."

That flicker of warmth flared to life within me. She didn't listen to him. She knew how to work a damn jack.

The woman grabbed the handle and began pumping, the arms extending slowly, inch by inch, pushing against the steel. The door groaned under the pressure, and the lock pulled tight, then twisted, straining against the moving pieces it was connected to. The metal frame shifted, and then the lock shattered with an abrasive snap.

She twisted the valve, folding the jack's arms neatly as they released. Kael pushed his mate behind him and forced the now-jammed door open. He stepped back, breathing hard, his gaze fixed on me. "Come on. And if you make one wrong move, I'll put you right back in there."

The door stood open, but my body refused to move. Every second of hunger, every ache and bruise, dragged me down. My paws scraped weakly against the concrete as I tried to lift myself, but the weight of exhaustion pinned me to the ground like chains.

Kael stood by the door, his patience like a storm about to break. "Come on, Destin. We don't have all night."

I pushed again, harder this time, my legs trembling under the effort. My claws scraped uselessly against the cold floor, and the room swayed around me. I hated this—hated being weak, hated having them see me like this. I snarled at the indignity, but there was nothing left to give.

Kael stepped forward, and his mate moved closer. Kael's expression hardened, his jaw clenching. "Stay back," he said, his voice a low warning. She stopped, tension radiating off her, but she obeyed.

The woman in black stood off to the side, arms crossed, her sharp gaze tracking my every movement. Watching me with pity.

I growled low in my throat and forced myself upright again. Pain screamed through my limbs, but I got one paw under me, then another. I loped on shaking legs to the door.

And then, Kael was no longer small. He stood, spreading his arms and legs, glowering down at me as he planted himself between me and the she-wolves. *Message received.*

He herded me like a sheep, and as my eyes adjusted to the light filtering from the upper level, I took in the stairs ahead of us. My body sagged. Impossible.

Kael crouched beside me, his arm reaching out, his hand landing on my pelt. I snapped my teeth at him—a weak attempt, but enough to make him jerk back. His face darkened with frustration. "You bite me, and I'll crush your jaw."

I snarled again, but it was all noise, no bite. Kael knew it, too. He grabbed my muzzle with a firm grip, squeezing just enough to get my attention. His voice was sharp now, all patience gone. "I'll drag you up by the scruff like a pup if I have to."

The indignity of it made my fur bristle, but my limbs were jelly beneath me, and I had no choice. I went still, my breath coming in shallow bursts through my nose. Satisfied, Kael let go of my muzzle and slid his arm under me, grunting with the effort.

He hauled me up, dragging my limp body toward the stairwell. Every muscle in my body screamed in protest, but Kael didn't stop, didn't slow.

"I can help." The woman in black strode toward us.

"No," Kael snapped, his voice clipped and sharp. "You stay with her."

The woman in black gave him a slow, measured look but said nothing. Just crossed her arms and waited. Kael cursed under his breath as he dragged me up the first step, then another. My claws scrabbled against the wood.

"Stop fighting me, damn it," Kael muttered through gritted teeth. His arm and shoulder trembled with the effort, but he didn't let go. He kept hauling me upward, step by painful step until the stairs finally ended, and the dim light of the exit glimmered ahead.

As soon as we hit solid ground, I wrenched myself free. My legs skittered awkwardly beneath me, but the wolf gave me just enough strength to stumble forward and through the door Kael slammed open, yelping at the bright sunlight.

The open air wrapped around me, sharp and cold, and it was like taking the first breath after drowning. I didn't look back. Didn't care about Kael or his mate or the woman in black. All that mattered was the forest—freedom. I struggled forward into the undergrowth, my paws hitting the soft earth like a heartbeat, the scent of pine and damp soil flooding my senses.

I needed to get far, far away from that place, but as I caught the scent of a rabbit, hunger caught me by the balls. I doubled back and lurched unsteadily, barely catching it between my jaws. Its bones snapped, the warm gush of blood coating my tongue as I tore into it. There was no hesitation, no thought—just survival.

I looked up from the kill, my eyes locking onto the woman in black again as she stood watching next to Kael and his mate. The taste of the rabbit filled my mouth, hot and metallic, but it wasn't enough. I wasn't sure anything ever would be. They didn't understand. They couldn't.

Kael waited for me to finish, then set down a small bucket,

emptied his water bottle into it, then tossed a set of clothes on the ground near me as I licked the blood from my muzzle. "When you're ready," he muttered, stepping back.

I ignored him, rushing to the bucket, desperately lapping up the water. When I thought I might be sick, I stumbled back, dropping onto my haunches. The food and water were already working their magic. Strength surged through me, making me heady.

I dropped to my belly, panting as relief flooded through me and, with it, clearer thoughts. I looked up and blinked. It was Kael in front of me. There weren't any alphas. Until proven otherwise, these wolves weren't my enemies.

I shifted in one fluid motion, bones snapping into place as fur receded. I didn't care about their stares. I pulled on the pants without ceremony but didn't bother with the shirt. I needed a bath. I wasn't going to ruin it with the week-old sweat, blood, and grime.

When I was decent, the woman in black stepped forward despite Kael's look of warning. There was that feeling again. That strange stillness. I hated it. It made my skin itch. "Do you know anything about Lava Forks?"

I blinked at her. *Lava Forks?* I'd been starved and beaten half to death, and she was asking me about the national forest? I turned and stalked into the trees.

"Destin," Kael called after me, and I heard the warning in his voice. He was like a son to me, and that tone made me want to knock him to the ground.

I turned. "I'm going back." My tongue was slow to form words. Thankfully, I didn't need to say more. He knew what I meant. I'd been kept here without any way to communicate with the wolves in my territory. They were loners and rogues, and they relied on my help.

"There's more at play here." Kael's eyes were dark.

"Did you give it back to them?" I asked. It would explain why the alphas were gone, though how it had taken Kael a week to find me—

"This is Lana. The dagger belongs to her." He pointed to the woman in black.

Lana. Her name echoed through me. She reached under the hem of her shirt and pulled the blade from a leather strap around her waist. "You know what this is?"

I spit on the ground at my feet. "That blade doesn't belong to anyone. You should melt it down. Destroy it.

"We found information about another relic." Lana spoke as if she hadn't heard me. "We think the alphas might be—"

"Destroy that, and they have nothing." My words came out sharp, slicing through the air between us.

Lana's eyes narrowed. "These relics aren't going away. If you know the prophecy—"

I turned back to the trees, not even waiting for her to finish. The relics, the prophecies, all of them, were only given for one purpose. Control. A way for packs to prove their value, their goodness. I didn't want any part of it.

I thought about turning back. About thanking them. But my feet kept moving forward into the trees, and I didn't try hard enough to stop them.

CHAPTER

FIVE

The silence Destin left behind swallowed everything. Leaves rustled in the breeze, the towering redwoods groaned, and the forest breathed around us. Destin's words clung to me like a thorn, sharp and lodged in my mind. My breath hitched, and I had to remind myself to exhale.

He'd been dragged through hell, and we expected him to stand there and answer our questions? Not asking. Demanding.

My stomach lurched at the image of his matted fur. The blood streaked over his bruised torso as he shifted. The pull of his golden eyes . . .

I shivered and reached into my jacket, pulling out the folded slip of paper.

Callista leaned in, scanning the faded lines. "It looks ancient."

My thumb traced the map's jagged lines, a bittersweet ache unfurling in my chest. *My brother would've loved this.* He'd spent entire summers mapping out make-believe treasure hunts as a kid.

Kael took the paper from my hands, scrutinizing it, then set it down and pulled out his phone. He showed us Lava Forks on a map. "Not too far."

"But we have no idea what we're looking for," I muttered.

"Or whether there will be others waiting." Callista chewed her lower lip. "How do you feel about a visit to Kootenay?" I didn't want to go crawling back to Rowan within days of us leaving, and Callista knew me well enough to understand that. She winced as she looked at me. "He talked with the witch. When he had the dagger. She might know something."

"The witch?" I raised an eyebrow.

Callista shrugged. "Unless you have a better idea?"

Rowan and Evelyn's house was exactly how I remembered it. As soon as I walked in, it felt like the air had been sucked out of my lungs. It had only been a couple of days, but the relief at entering a place that was so familiar made pressure build behind my eyes.

Callista and Kael had gone to her brother Blake's house as soon as they got back into town, then let me take the truck. For a brief moment, I thought about stopping back home. At my two-bedroom ranch with the raspberry bushes out front and the sliced cheese, lettuce, and lunch meat that was still waiting in my refrigerator.

I couldn't do it. Not when I knew deep in my soul that this hunt was taking me anywhere but back home. I'd have to go there tonight to sleep, but I was putting it off as long as possible.

I trudged into the kitchen, only realizing as I sat down on one of the wooden chairs that I hadn't heard from or felt my wolf since we'd left to drive back home. Instead of staying another night in the hotel, we took turns driving and sleeping and returned in record time.

Rowan leaned back against the wall across from me as Evelyn sat. He scanned my face like he was trying to read my thoughts. I pulled the folded paper out of my pocket and set it on the table, then smoothed the edges.

And then I told them everything.

The building had been empty. The alphas were gone. According to this snippet, they had information on another relic that was possibly hidden somewhere in the mountains. Rowan's gaze darkened. Evelyn let out a low breath.

When I finished, I tapped my fingers on the table. "Callista said you might know . . . a witch?"

Rowan chuckled and rubbed the back of his neck. "Lyra. She lives out in the woods. Runs a mushroom farm."

"How does a witch end up being a mushroom farmer?" Evelyn crossed her arms. "I mean, of all things."

Rowan smirked. "Dark, damp, a bit mysterious."

Evelyn's lips twitched. "And you think she'll know something about this?"

He shrugged. "She knew about the dagger. You saw that firsthand."

Evelyn exhaled. "She didn't like it. I doubt she'll be happy to see it again." Her eyes moved to my hip where the leather strap was visible.

My hand dropped involuntarily. "If she didn't like it, she may not like me." I looked up at Rowan. "Maybe you should go."

He shook his head. "No. She didn't share everything with us last time. Maybe she needs to see the prophecy isn't just words." Rowan met my eyes. "The packs are agitated. With the alphas missing—"

"They know about that already?"

He nodded. "I told them as soon as you called. I had to."

I pursed my lips. Of course he had to. We didn't know for a fact that the alphas were still up north. We suspected, but we couldn't withhold information based on a hypothesis.

"They know something is happening, and it's making them restless. I need to get a message out to the others, increase our patrols. See if we can find anything before this whole thing spirals out of control," Rowan finished.

Guilt pressed against my chest. I should've been out there helping Rowan keep everything together. But instead, I was on this wild hunt for relics, two steps behind.

Rowan moved to stand behind Evelyn and dropped his hands on her shoulders. "Meet us tomorrow morning. We'll drive to Lyra together. It'll go better if we're all there."

I nodded, hesitating. I knew what came next, and I was still in denial. Evelyn offered me a cup of tea, and I took it. She told me about visiting Will's pup, and by the time I emptied my mug and walked to the door, I felt the slightest bit less dead inside.

I slipped behind the wheel of Kael's truck and took the long way home. The weight of the past few days sat heavily on my shoulders, pressing against me with every kilometer. I didn't feel like myself. I was drifting, unmoored.

I passed the school, slowing as I drove by. This was supposed to be my time to prepare for the new term. I should've been sitting in meetings, collaborating with other teachers, and getting ready for my students. Instead, I was chasing ancient prophecies without guarantee they'd lead anywhere.

For some reason, seeing the school pushed my mind to Kael. How he'd been abandoned by his pack when his body hadn't presented perfectly. Then, my thoughts drifted to Destin. I shook my head, trying to shake the memory of the feral way he'd stared at us, all teeth and claws, more animal than man. He had been in bad shape, but somehow, even in that state, he had kept going. No pack, no structure, no one to rely on. Just himself.

What kind of life was that? It was something I couldn't imagine. A wolf without a pack? I'd always been surrounded by people—first my family, then my pack. Without that, I wouldn't have survived after my brother's death.

Humans needed other humans, but more than that, wolves needed other wolves.

I swiped a tear from my cheek. I felt like a guest in my own life. And if I wasn't part of Black Lake or Kootenay anymore, where did that leave me? Was it possible to be a part of two packs? To still have a place in one while I searched for the other?

I wound through the familiar curves of town, the lights dimming as I pulled into my driveway. Home. I parked the truck and stared at the little two-bedroom ranch in front of me, exactly as I'd left it. That was more of a gut punch than if I'd found it torn apart.

I climbed out of the truck and went to the front door, unlocking it with a click. Inside, the house was still and quiet, the scent still familiar. The same pile of shoes sat by the door. The same throw blanket was draped over the arm of the couch.

I locked the door behind me, twisting the bolt into place with more force than necessary. I grabbed a drink of water from the tap, then checked the windows, double-checked the door, and flicked off the lights before heading to my room.

I quickly washed my face and brushed my teeth, grabbing a spare toothbrush rather than unpacking my toiletries. The bed greeted me with familiar sheets, still soft from the last time I'd washed them. But when I crawled under the covers, exhaustion clinging to every part of me, sleep was slow to come.

After tossing and turning, then staring at the backs of my eyelids for what felt like an hour, I flicked on my light and pulled my bag closer to the bed. I dug through it and found the book I'd taken from the desk and thumbed through the pages. It was an illustrated version. Beautiful.

Every story held more meaning after hearing Kael's friend, Bill, talk about it. I shivered, remembering how the dagger had claimed him. It felt better to state it that way instead of admitting it had been my hand that wielded it.

I flipped to the end and started reading.

THERE ONCE WAS a man named Thorne Moreau, a brilliant dreamer with a heart divided between fierce love for his friends and the dark whisper of the cursed dagger. The dagger craved blood, and soon, so did Thorne, wielding it not just to protect those he cared for, but to punish anyone who dared cross him. As his ambitions grew, Thorne sought the ancient relics, magical artifacts said to grant limitless power. One by one, he claimed them, and for a moment, he stood on the edge of building an empire where no one could challenge him. But power has its price. The relics, united in his grasp, betrayed him —turning their magic inward, unraveling his mind like threads of a forgotten tapestry. Lost to madness, Thorne was left grasping at shadows, and the relics slipped from his control, scattering themselves to the farthest corners of the world, waiting for the next soul bold—or foolish—enough to seek them.

. . .

I inspected the dark illustrations of a wolf driven mad, and my eyelids finally began to droop. Setting the book on my night-stand, I turned off the lamp and sank into my pillow.

That was my heritage. Thorne, if not my ancestor, was the alpha of my family line. He'd been corrupted by the relics and paid the price. But was it possible for someone, anyone, to stay sane with that much power at their disposal? Was it the man who failed or the relics?

I drove over to Callista's first thing in the morning so we could arrive early at the meeting spot. The air was crisp, but after being up north, it felt like the middle of summer. The leaves were barely beginning to change.

Rowan and Evelyn pulled up, and we exchanged silent nods. Kael was back in the driver's seat, and he followed them back onto the highway. We drove for around forty-five minutes before parking on a side road. We each grabbed our packs, then walked into the cover of trees so we could shift.

The transformation was always a rush, a flood of sensation as my senses heightened. My vision sharpened, colors became more vibrant, and the sounds of the forest grew louder. The rustle of leaves in the breeze, the scuttle of small animals in the underbrush. All of it broadcast through my head.

The cool earth pressed against my paws as I stood, my wolf form powerful and ready. I exhaled with relief. Even though I hadn't heard a peep from my wolf, she was still there. I wanted to ask why she'd been so quiet, but I had learned not to push. We'd talk when she was ready and not before.

With a silent agreement, we set off, the four of us moving

as one through the forest, carrying our packs with our teeth. The run was exhilarating, the wind rushing past my fur, but I couldn't quite shed the undercurrent of nerves. What if Lyra knew nothing? That was more terrifying than her being angry at seeing me and the dagger.

I pushed harder, my muscles straining as I kept pace with Rowan at the front. He'd always been fast. I was quicker at maneuvering, but it was difficult to beat him in an outright sprint.

We reached the edge of the clearing where Lyra's farm lay, and we slowed to a halt. One by one, we dropped our packs and shifted, our bodies snapping back to our human forms. I shivered as I pulled on my clothes and strapped the dagger to my hip.

I didn't know what I'd been expecting. Maybe a cottage nestled between the trees, its stone walls covered in ivy. That was not what I was looking at. In front of us was a low building with commercial siding. "This is it?" I asked. Rowan nodded and led us to the door.

Lyra was waiting for us behind a long counter. At least she looked exactly as a witch should. Delicate features, her hair almost silver, it was so light. Her eyes glinted with an unnerving, knowing look.

Her gaze froze when it landed on me. She leaned over the counter, resting on her arms. "This is different," she said, her voice low and resonant. "It's taken to you, hasn't it?"

I blinked, then noticed my hand was resting over the dagger.

Lyra's eyes narrowed, and the air seemed to grow thicker. "My question is . . . why?"

Rowan cleared his throat. "You told us of the legend. About the five relics."

"I did. I told you their power was too much for one to wield. And yet you come here searching for another?"

I swallowed hard. "No." Her violet eyes flicked to mine, and my pulse sped. It wasn't often that I felt intimidated, but Lyra made the blood in my veins run cold. "I mean, yes, but not because we want them. Because we don't want them to fall into the wrong hands."

"And your hands are the right ones?" Lyra raised an eyebrow.

My fingers tensed. "I'm Shadow Pack." The words slipped out, and when Kael's expression darkened, I winced, wishing I could take them back.

Lyra's mouth curled at the edges. "Yes. And that is both a blessing and a curse."

Callista shivered next to me. I thought of the wound on her arm. The way the dagger had consumed me at the pool. The blade held my blood, and while it felt calm and docile, I could never forget what it felt like when it hungered.

I pulled out the piece of paper from my pack and handed it to her. She already knew about the relics and my blood, so there wasn't any point keeping it from her.

Lyra's eyes scrolled over the words, and her smirk spread into a full smile. "Oh, of course!" She laughed out loud, the sound high and tinkling.

"You know this place?" My heart began to speed.

Lyra sobered. "No. There is only one wolf I know of who has explored that site. And he almost gave his life for it." Kael stiffened next to me. I turned with a questioning look as Lyra raised an eyebrow. She leaned further over the counter. "You know of whom I speak?"

Kael looked from Lyra to the four of us. He opened his mouth, then closed it.

Lyra seemed delighted by this response. "If you can get him to help you, please come back and report. I haven't seen that handsome rogue in far too long."

CHAPTER
SIX

DESTIN

My cabin sat nestled against the trees, its logs darkened by years, storms, and seasons. It looked solid. Sturdy. Almost like it had sprung out of the ground one day. Truthfully, it almost had.

Autumn pressed close, the air sharp and dry with the promise of frost, though winter hadn't yet sunk its claws in. The forest shifted around me, the steady hum of life preparing for the cold months ahead. Everything followed instinct out here—hunt, store, survive. I belonged in it, moving through the motions like any other creature carving out its place.

My axe waited on the stump where I'd been about to use it when the alphas came for me. My traps had worked on two of them. Not the third. Rage flashed through me at the memory, and I grabbed the tool.

The rhythm of the swing came easy. A brutal, repetitive

thud against the wood. Logs split beneath the blade, the scent of sap rising on the air. My muscles burned with the strain— good pain. Pain that reminded me I was alive, here, free. Not stuck lapping up my own blood off of concrete.

I stacked up the firewood beside the cabin, neat and solid. A fortress against the coming cold. Every log added was one step closer to making it through the season, one less reason to leave the safety of this place. I made my world simple. Keep warm, keep fed, help others. Anything more was trouble.

Each swing sent a jolt through my arms, and memories rode the edge of every impact. Not the warehouse, not the alphas with their twisted grins. No. It was older than that. Wolves breaking beneath an alpha's gaze, bones snapping when submission didn't come fast enough. The pack. *My pack.*

Seeing Kael again opened up a lock box of memories that I thought I'd long since buried. The past clawed at me, and I swung harder, splitting the log clean in two. The crack of wood echoed through the clearing.

The wind kicked up, threading between the trees and pulling at my jacket. The air whispered of the cold waiting just over the ridge. I shivered once, not from the chill but from the thought of being caught unprepared. I only had a few hours, and then I needed to start on my rounds. I didn't have weeks to give, but that was what the northern alphas had stolen from me.

I pulled the axe free from the stump, wiping sweat from my brow as the sun dipped low, sending shadows stretching long across the clearing. I balanced a log on my shoulder and headed back toward the cabin.

Another flash. Lava Forks. The disappointment in my old alpha's eyes. The ground rumbling beneath my feet. It didn't matter how many years passed, that sensation of being completely and utterly powerless stayed with me, biting deeper every time I remembered.

My wolf stirred, restless inside me. He wasn't used to sitting back, but I had my task list for the week. Reinforce the cabin walls. Fix the roof where a branch had dropped a few weeks prior. Traps—check the traps. Always the traps. Everything had to be ready before the snow came, before the mountain locked us in for good.

My wolf didn't care about roofs or firewood. His needs were simpler. Eat, sleep, fight. *Mate.* That last one lingered longer than it should have. I'd always met my needs—found what I required when the urge struck, but I'd never taken a mate. Never wanted one. It was easier that way. Cleaner.

A low growl rumbled inside me, and I pushed my wolf back. No, I hissed. He was singularly obsessed with Lana. The woman in black. He'd noticed her right away—too much fire, too much fight. Dangerous. He liked that. Wanted to know what she'd taste like, how her skin would feel under his teeth.

I shifted the log on my shoulder, jaw tightening. He couldn't think past the fact that she smelled different—wild. Strong. Like she didn't belong to anyone. I exhaled, my jeans tightening as I threw the log down. *Not helpful,* I grunted.

And then the wind shifted, and her scent whispered through the trees. I ground my teeth. If this was another memory—

No. Another scent. Kael's.

My senses heightened, taking in every shift in the air, every twitch of a branch. I felt the thud of paws on damp earth, the soft scrape of claws against roots. They came in wolf form, bodies low and quick. *Kael.* He didn't belong here, not anymore. He'd made his choice to leave and now to be a pack wolf.

He'd brought his mate and the woman in black. She smelled like rain on dry earth. My wolf whimpered.

When they stopped just beyond the tree line, they shifted. The crack of bone, the slide of muscle beneath skin. Years in the woods had dulled the spectacle for me. Shifting wasn't something to gawk at. It was just survival. But I had a difficult time convincing my eyes to stay on the wood pile knowing *she* was there in the trees.

Kael emerged first, his shoulders tense. His mate followed, pulling on a jacket and rubbing her arms against the chill. The other woman appeared last, moving with a confidence that scraped against my senses. Her steps were sure, her stance strong. She didn't seem to care about the cold. Her breath drifted in clouds, but she stood still as stone, eyes scanning the clearing like she belonged here. My wolf stirred—too interested, too aware of her presence. I moved back to the chopping block.

Kael stepped forward, gaze cautious. "Took a while to find you up here. I forgot how far back this place is."

I shrugged. *Isolation was the point.* Kael knew that, which meant he was saying that for his mate's benefit. He was probably trying to impress her. Avoiding talking about the truth we both knew. That this had been his home. He'd always planned on staying a lone wolf just like me.

I turned back toward the axe embedded in the stump. They could say their piece, and then they could leave.

Kael's eyes drifted to the traps scattered along the edge of the clearing. "Still using the same tricks."

I nodded. "They work."

He chuckled. "Only if you don't know they're there."

His mate turned in a circle. "You grew up here?"

I stiffened, then balanced a log and swung the axe harder than necessary. A few moments later, Kael and his mate stood next to me. "This is Callista." He gestured toward her, and she grinned like she hadn't spent a day of her life suffering. "And this is Lana."

I gave them both a nod—enough acknowledgment to be polite, not enough to invite conversation—and returned to my work.

Kael picked up a log and stacked it next to my block. He didn't ask. Just worked. I leveled him with a stare, waving him off with a quick jerk of my hand. "I don't need your help."

Kael walked to the scrap pile and hoisted another log without missing a beat. "I know."

His mate moved to join him, but Kael stopped her with a glance. "Stay back. It's cold. No reason to—"

She shook him off, sorting through the pile to find a solid piece. Lana stopped on the opposite side, far enough back that she wouldn't be hit with flying wood, then gathered the pieces I split and carried them to the stack behind us. I glowered at the three of them.

"What's the problem?" she asked. "You don't want help, or you don't want help from she-wolves?"

I grunted. Let her believe whatever the hell she wanted to about me. Her animosity would only make things easier. I swung my axe, and as she bent to collect the pieces, her scent moved like a wave, wrapping around me.

I jerked my chin toward the shed. "The kindling needs moving."

Lana's eyes flashed. "Fine." She set the pieces on the stack, then stalked across the yard.

I swung. I split. Kael and Callista moved wood until the sun had dipped far below the trees, and I was covered in sweat.

Kael wiped his hand on his jeans, and his breath fogged in the cooling air. "Think that's enough?"

I gave a curt nod, jerking my chin toward the cabin. "There's food inside."

Kael raised an eyebrow. "You mean you aren't a total misanthrope?"

The corner of my mouth twitched, but I shoved the reaction down. "Don't get used to it."

The scent of meat and woodsmoke clung to the cabin, wrapping tight in the warm air that settled over the hearth. I hadn't planned on visitors, but I had plenty of stored vegetables in my root cellar to expand the stew I'd started earlier that morning.

The fire crackled, snapping with small bursts of flame as I stirred the pot. Meat and roots, simple food I could trust. My wolf preferred it that way.

"You need help serving?" Kael's voice cut through the silence, too casual. Too much like he belonged here.

I shook my head. "I've got it."

I spooned the stew into bowls, the earthy smell rising with the steam. Kael was already moving, his presence loud and close. I handed one off with a grunt, avoiding his gaze. He handed it to his mate, then came back for his. I couldn't tell if I was glad for him.

Lana took her bowl without a word, but as her finger brushed mine, she flinched, nearly sloshing the broth over the lip of the dish. She pursed her lips and retreated faster than a rabbit sensing a wolf.

Kael dug into his bowl without ceremony, spoon scraping loudly against the ceramic. Callista—his mate—tore bread into pieces and dipped them into the stew, her expression soft with contentment.

Lana swirled her spoon in the broth, her dark eyes flicking between the three of us. She took a sip, slow and deliberate. "This is good," she said, her tone guarded.

Callista nodded, mouth full of bread. "Better than good. You've got skills, Destin."

I hunched my shoulders, turning my focus to the stew in my own bowl. "It's just food." Words felt clunky in my mouth, too human. Too much effort.

Kael scoffed. "He's always been a good cook."

"You made this?" Lana dipped her bread into the stew, chewing slowly.

I nodded once. The air between us felt strange, off-balance. It was time to get this over with. I scraped my chair back from the table, the sound sharp against the quiet. "You didn't come here to rate my cooking. What do you want?"

I didn't need to ask the question. They'd already started this conversation outside of my cell. They were disillusioned if they thought they were going to give me a few days and catch me in a better moment.

Kael set his spoon down, his expression sobering. "I wanted to make sure you were good."

"I'm good." I folded my arms across my chest.

Kael glanced up with a look that said, *can you stop being an asshole for five seconds?*

I sent one back that said, *probably not.* He knew me better than anyone. He knew I wouldn't like him bringing people here even if he trusted them.

"Great. Well. Thanks for dinner." Kael slurped down the last of his stew, then pushed his chair back.

Lana put out a hand and stopped him. "Uh, no." She turned to me, her eyes flashing. "You were like a father to him. He risked his life to free you from that hell hole, and you're going to sit here and pretend—"

"Lana." Kael blew out a breath.

"You might have respect for him, but I don't," she snapped. "You haven't even said thank you."

I clenched my jaw. "Thank you."

She rolled her eyes and stood. "Maybe there's more than one reason you live alone in the woods."

The growl came unbidden, curling up from my chest. I stood, fists clenched at my sides. "You don't know me."

Lana whirled, still holding her bowl. "I think I know enough." She stalked to the kitchen counter, rinsed her bowl and set it in the sink. Kael and his mate sat stock still across from me.

The itch to run clawed at me, instinct pulling me toward the door, toward the safety of solitude. Kael stood, his hand raised in some kind of peace offering. "We just want to understand, Destin. If you know something—"

"You're a coward." Lana charged back to the table, staring me straight in the eyes. "You can't even hear him out. You sit here in your cabin in the woods not giving a shit what happens to anyone past your damn perimeter—"

"*I care.*" My voice echoed off the walls, and the cabin stilled. My wolf surged, teeth bared in my mind.

Lana's eyes locked with mine, fierce and unwavering. "Then prove it."

I stepped toward her, my wolf prowling just beneath the surface. "You have no idea what I do for the wolves in my territory. You know nothing of the suffering they've endured—"

She stepped forward, stabbing a finger into my chest. "I lost my brother. Watched him die while I stood there, helpless. I work with kids daily whose brains and bodies bind them in a prison worse than the one we just kindly removed you from." Her words hit like claws raking across my ribs. She wasn't backing down, and my wolf didn't know what to do with that. "So don't talk to me about suffering."

Lana's chest rose and fell with shallow breaths, and then

she turned and stormed out the door. The slam reverberated in the silence.

Kael's gaze weighed heavy, but I shoved away from the table, the need to move overwhelming. I was out the door before I realized it, the cold air sharp against my skin.

Lana's figure cut through the clearing, her steps fast and deliberate, and my wolf lunged forward, driving me after her. "Lana!" The word ripped from my throat, but she kept going, her dark hair catching the wind.

Then a sharp sting cut against the skin of my neck. I grunted and stumbled back, searching for whatever had snapped against me, but the sensation didn't lessen. It only burned hotter the more I moved.

When I looked up, Lana was there in front of me. "I recommend you hold still. Unless you don't want to be able to shift for the foreseeable future."

CHAPTER
SEVEN

Lana

I crouched on the soft mulch in front of Destin's steps. I'd been methodical, setting up the trap exactly as I'd seen it done when we approached. The filament was sharp to the touch, notched in a way that if it was pulled, it would dig deeper into the skin. I didn't know exactly what plant he'd used to coat it, but Kael had said it was some kind of natural poison. One that would keep a shifter from shifting. I needed more of that in my possession.

Now the trap was cinched around Destin's neck. The porch banister had made it easy for me to lift it up without notice while Destin was busy in the kitchen. He let out a low growl and tugged, but the filament only tightened, digging into his skin. "Son of a bitch!" he spat, his voice rough and filled with fury.

"Good evening." I stood and brushed dirt off my knees. "Fancy seeing you out here."

His eyes burned with anger, and he yanked harder against the trap. "Let me out of this, Lana."

I exhaled. "You know my name. I wasn't sure until you yelled it like a curse word." Destin seethed, and I shook my head. "I'm not letting you out until you tell me what I want to know."

I was fairly sure he was going to allow the barbs to rip through his skin at some point. Even if he didn't shift, he had mass and strength on his side. I pulled the dagger and held it out between us. "Don't test me." I wasn't going to use it, but he didn't have to know that.

Destin's hands balled into fists as he glared at me. His breath came in short puffs. He let out a low laugh but didn't speak. His eyes were wild, his wolf so close to the surface, they shone.

"Don't want to talk? I think I have a better chance than those alphas did." I stepped closer, the dried leaves crunching under my boots. Kael and Callista were still inside, and I was glad. I didn't want Kael feeling sorry for his feral mentor.

I stopped in front of him, just far enough that his arms couldn't reach without pulling on the thread. "They had one of the relics, Destin. This dagger? They were planning to use it to kill wolves in the area. They wanted to use our blood to control the packs." I pointed back to the house. "I'm pretty sure you already know that, though. I heard Kael talking with you on the phone."

Destin's jaw clenched. "And you think I give a damn about relics or alphas?"

I took another step closer, my heart pounding in my chest. "It doesn't matter if you care about relics or alphas. They're coming for us whether we like it or not. If we don't find them first, we'll be at their mercy."

He scoffed. "And you think you can stop them?"

I nodded, my gaze steady. "I think we have a better chance if we work together." I paused, searching his eyes. "Look, I don't know what brought you up here, what made you turn your back on the packs, but I was mostly trying to piss you off in there. Kael talks about you like you're a god. He helped deliver a baby in our pack because of the training you gave him, so I'm not going to pretend like all of this is the extent of who you are. I don't think you're a coward."

Destin's expression hardened. "You don't know anything about me."

"I don't need to know anything other than the fact that you want to help the wolves here," I said, my voice softening. "Help me see how doing nothing will accomplish that because right now, all I see is a pack I need to protect. And wolves in this area that are going to be caught in the crossfire. If you have a better vision of how this is all going to go down, then tell me."

He didn't answer, his eyes locked on mine. The silence stretched between us.

"I'd be happy to leave you tied up out here." I crossed my arms over my chest to keep him from seeing my trembling fingers. Trapping him had been a risk, but everything I'd seen from him told me he was all instinct. I needed to speak his language. Strength. Stubbornness. Two things I was relatively good at.

Kael and Callista's voices carried out from the cabin, and I turned my head. They were standing in the doorway, their expressions a mix of confusion and curiosity.

"What's going on out here?" Kael called. He stepped out onto the porch, his breath fogging in the air. "Why is Destin all trussed up like a Christmas ham?"

Callista's eyes widened. "Is that—?" She glanced to the perimeter of the trees. "When did you—?"

"It doesn't matter," I muttered.

Kael smirked, the corners of his mouth twitching. "I didn't realize you were into bondage, Lana."

"Shut the hell up, Kael."

Callista gave him a long look. "Are you forgetting she did the same thing to you?" Kael's neck reddened.

I focused back on Destin. "Just tell me about Lava Forks. Then we'll march out of your life and leave you to your log splitting."

"I can't tell you. It's something I'd have to show you." Destin stopped fighting the filament, but his muscles still tensed.

"What is it?"

He ground his teeth. "A sacred site."

Yeah, nothing new there. "And you know this because?"

Kael pushed off the doorframe. "That doesn't matter."

I looked between the two of them. It didn't matter, but my curiosity was piqued.

"I'll take you there. It's more than a full day's journey. Then you're on your own."

Hope bubbled up in my chest, but I didn't let it show. "How do I know you'll keep your word?"

"He'll keep his word. He's a stubborn ass, but he does what he says." Kael pulled Callista into his side.

I stepped up to Destin. "Hold still."

He glared at me as I reached for the filament, my fingers brushing against his coat. I lifted the catch, and the filament loosened. I wasn't going to cut it and ruin a perfectly good trap.

Destin didn't move as I rolled the thread into a loose lasso. Warmth from his body seeped into me, and I stepped back. He muttered something under his breath and turned back toward the cabin. "You'll have to stay here for the night." He stormed past Kael and Callista.

Touchy.

I followed them inside where a dim light from a single oil lamp cast shadows across the room. The furnishings were minimal, no clutter, no excess. Destin knelt next to a trunk and pulled out a few quilts and blankets, then a rolled-up mat that looked like it had seen better days. "This is what I've got." He stood and handed them to Kael, his eyes meeting mine for a brief moment before he looked away.

Kael nodded, taking the supplies. "Thanks."

"You two can take your old room. If you want." Destin looked at a set of narrow stairs at the end of the room leading to a loft.

Kael glanced at me, and I nodded. He'd hear if anything went down overnight.

Destin turned and walked out of the room and down the hall to what I presumed was his bedroom. I took the mat and bedding from Kael, then found a spot near the fire. Callista handed me my pack. We'd brought them inside, but I'd completely forgotten about them.

She and Kael used the guest bathroom first, then escaped to the loft. I took my toiletries into the room, surprised that there was any kind of running water. Sure, I had to use a pump to get fresh water in the sink and the same to fill a bucket to flush the toilet, but it was better than walking to an outhouse.

Questions swirled in my head. Had Destin built this place? Had he dug a well? Built a septic system? Regardless of whether I was convinced he was crazy, it was impressive. And it was a stark contrast to my life with the pack, where there was plenty of luxury and comfort. *Or had been.* What did that say about Destin? About me?

My mind buzzed with the events of the day as I brushed my teeth, and I couldn't help but replay my conversation with Destin over and over. He hadn't said anything to the alphas. He'd let them beat the shit out of him, but he hadn't divulged his secret. *Why?* It was stupid. He didn't care about any of it. He could've talked and gone back to his solitary life in the woods, but instead, he'd taken the abuse and kept his mouth shut.

Maybe they wouldn't have let him go. Maybe they were waiting for Kael, regardless.

My thoughts spiraled. What if the alphas decided to go ahead without him? Had they already sent wolves to Lava Rock? My gut twisted at the thought of them finding something before we did—something powerful enough to shift the balance of power in their favor.

Tomorrow. We'd find out at least some of the answers then.

My thoughts wandered back to Destin. What had happened to him? Kael had protected him when I brought up Lava Rock. What had driven him to live alone in the mountains, to fashion traps and keep people at more than arm's length? Had he been betrayed? Abandoned like Kael? Or had he chosen this life, casting off the bonds of pack and family for reasons only he understood?

I blew out a breath and closed my eyes, trying to shut off my racing thoughts. I needed to be ready for whatever came next. For the alphas and their power plays. For the secrets Lava Rock might reveal.

I stalked back into the room, settling next to the crackling fire. I lay down on the mat and pulled the blanket over me, but my mind still raced. I reached for my pack and pulled out the book, turning to the same page I'd read earlier.

. . .

THERE ONCE WAS a man named Thorne Moreau . . . One by one, he claimed them . . . But power has its price . . . Lost to madness.

WHAT HAD HE DONE? I turned back, taking in the swirling color and the goblet that lay at the center of it. I read the subtitle.

THE MATE OF THORNE MOREAU, once stricken with disease, then revived with wine from the everlasting goblet.

MUST BE NICE. I flipped back, this time finding another picture of Thorne, a gilded crown sitting atop his head.

THE ALPHA AND THE CROWN. No wolf's mind is his or her own.

I FROWNED. What the hell kind of kid's storybook was this? I closed the book and set it aside, then flicked off the lamp. My muscles began to relax, and I almost drifted off when I felt a twinge in my bladder. *Damn it.* Had I forgotten to use the toilet or had I drunk too much at dinner? I groaned and pushed off the blankets and made my way across the room, careful not to disturb Kael or Callista.

The cabin was dimly lit, the only illumination coming from the flickering flames and the soft glow of the oil lamp on the table. I found the hallway and turned the corner, my eyes adjusting to the dark.

I was halfway to the bathroom when I heard a rustling sound and looked up. My breath caught in my throat. Destin stood in his room past the open door, his back to me, shirtless.

He must have just come from the bathroom. I hadn't heard anything in the hall, but—

His muscles flexed as he pulled a shirt over his head. His skin was taut over defined muscle, and his shoulders were broad, tapering down to a narrow waist. I tried to rip my eyes away, but couldn't. Slightly different than that day in the woods when he was emaciated.

My wolf let out a low hum, and I almost laughed. Days of nothing from her, and now she was wide awake? *Down girl.* I finally succeeded in forcing myself to look away, then slipped into the bathroom.

My heart pounded in my chest as I stood there, staring at the porcelain sink. *What the hell, Lana?* It was just a body. Just a very nice, very attractive body that I'd never seen before. Even though I'd seen him shift outside of the alpha's building, he looked nothing like that. He'd healed. Grown strong again. And it was a sight to behold.

I pumped water and splashed it on my face, trying to cool the sudden heat that had risen to my cheeks. I took a deep breath, then reached for the towel hanging on the rack. I nearly forgot to use the toilet, but thankfully remembered at the last second. I relieved myself, then washed my hands and dried them.

I opened the door and stepped back into the hall, tiptoeing to my bed. I needed to stay focused. To keep my eyes on the prize.

Not on Destin's muscular back.

CHAPTER

EIGHT

The bed was a mess when I woke up. Sheets tangled and twisted, the pillow halfway across the room. I must've thrashed around like a wild animal.

An apt description.

I dreamed of her. Or my wolf did. One of the two. Either way, images of Lana beneath me played through my mind's eye as I threw on clothes and silently made my way out the front door. I peeked at Lana on my way through. She was still asleep on her cot. Her dark hair splayed out over her pillow.

That wasn't helping.

I stepped out onto the porch and sucked in a breath of crisp morning air. Going for a run in human form wasn't something I usually did, but I was so full of restless energy I thought I might burst out of my skin.

I took off, heading for my favorite trail through the trees. As

53

my pulse quickened, I considered the day ahead of me. I'd stop by a few wolves on our way north, then take Lana to the site. We wouldn't drive. Too obvious, and there weren't good roads up there anyway. Hopefully, she was up for some long runs on her paws and a night or two spent under the stars.

The thought of seeing her in wolf form nearly made me stumble on an exposed branch. I was suddenly desperate to know what she looked like. What color of fur she had.

I ran faster. I ran until my saliva tasted metallic at the back of my throat, then looped back to the cabin. Since there was still no sign of life inside, I switched into my boots and walked to the shed to retrieve my toolbox. The morning air was crisp, biting at my exposed skin. I walked around to the side of the cabin where an eave hung crookedly, one of the hinges barely attached. I grabbed my ladder from the back and went up with my drill.

The metal was icy against my skin, and I had to blow on my hands to warm them up. I worked the screws loose, the old metal protesting with a screech. I reshaped it, forcing it back into place, then put in extra screws to reinforce it.

I packed away my tools, satisfied, and walked around to the front of the cabin. Kael, Callista, and Lana were all in the main room, sitting around the table. Lana's eyes were half-lidded as she gazed at the steaming mug before her.

I stepped inside and closed the door behind me.

"Morning." Kael nodded, then returned to talking with Callista. I hung my coat on the rack and tugged off my boots, but my eyes were glued to the woman sitting across the table.

Lana looked like she hadn't slept any better than I had. Dark circles under her eyes, a furrow in her brow that hadn't been there the night before. My wolf pawed in my head, drawing my attention to her and her alone. A movement of her hands, a flicker of emotion in her eyes. My skin prickled as my instincts sharpened, noting how her chair was turned away from Callista and Kael.

She lifted her mug to her lips and took a sip, her eyes flicking up to mine, then away again. My wolf growled, but I shoved him back. It wasn't a surprise that she kept her distance, but my chest squeezed at the loneliness sinking inside her. I felt it. The emptiness. The black hole that couldn't be filled.

My psi abilities allowed me to feel everything. Whether I wanted to or not.

She needed an outlet, someone to let her vent or just sit with her in silence, and I wanted . . . I wanted to be that person. But that was how I'd gotten into trouble with my pack. Always trying to fix things. Always trying to be the one people turned to.

I couldn't let people come to me. I had to go to them.

I clenched my fists, my nails digging into my palms. I couldn't do it. She was temporary, moving through on her search for the relics. I had a place. I was needed here.

I was already too close to the wolves who lived near me. I was the one who helped with their injuries, listened to their complaints, and made sure they had what they needed. I was their fixer. But I wasn't their friend. I couldn't afford to be. I'd learned that too many times the hard way.

What I could do was offer her coffee. Or breakfast. Anything to ease the tension in my chest. "Want more?" I motioned to the empty pot still sitting on the stove.

Lana shook her head, and my wolf huffed in disappointment.

Kael looked between the two of us, his eyes narrowing. "What do you know about the northern alpha?"

Tension curled up my spine. I knew what he was asking, but I wasn't going there. "Not much."

Kael's gaze was steady. "They were masking their scent."

I breathed, working to keep my expression even. "Huh."

"There aren't many wolves who can do that." His voice was low. Calm. His mate had no idea what he was communicating behind those words.

The past clawed at the back of my mind, memories I'd long since tried to bury. Kael thought he knew about that alpha. The one who had left him. The one Kael believed was his father.

Kael wasn't the kind to spill his soul. He was young when I'd found him, and his story had come out in pieces between drinks and the rare moments we weren't focused on surviving. That bastard was the reason for everything wrong in his life. He'd abandoned him, left him broken and unwanted. Given him the same abilities.

The question wasn't whether I should tell him. It was whether I could. Whether I wanted to throw a wrench into everything Kael had managed to build with that truth. Kael thought his old alpha was dead. Probably because that's what I'd told him when he was a teen. What would it do to him, to his mate, if I dragged that ghost into the light?

My wolf shifted uneasily under my skin, pacing in my mind. I'd always been good at handling instinct—knowing when to fight and when to keep my head down. But maybe I'd chosen wrong with him.

I cleared my throat. "I thought you met with them."

"Only one," Kael answered.

If I told him, he'd hate me for it. If I kept quiet, he'd hate me anyway, eventually. "I think we've all picked up some tricks."

Kael's jaw tightened, the muscle ticking once, twice. "Not many tricks like that."

His mate glanced between us, sensing the tension but staying quiet. Smart. She knew when to stay out of it. But Kael wasn't going to let this drop, not now. I could see it in his eyes —the gears turning, the questions forming. He was chasing a scent, and soon enough, he'd catch it.

I weighed my options, the silence stretching too long between us. My wolf nudged at the edge of my thoughts. "It's him," I said finally.

He was quiet for a beat. "And yours?"

I nodded, anger boiling in my chest.

Callista leaned forward. "Both of your alphas are part of this alliance?" For the first time, something fiery and hot burned in her eyes. Her disgust and rage flared, hitting me in the gut. She put a hand over Kael's. "We have to find them."

"We have to find the relic." Lana's hand sat on the dagger she kept at her hip. "We don't know if they're in the same location, and without something to track—"

"Evelyn." Callista turned to Kael. "She tracked you. Even though you masked your scent, she still found your trail."

Lana straightened. "Do you think she'll come?"

Callista shrugged. "Not without Rowan."

Lana's brow furrowed. "He'll come. He's desperate to help the packs, and finding the alpha alliance would be the highest form of protection."

"What about the pack?" Callista asked.

Lana's words were sharp. "He has Jasper and your brother. He has Tori and Mara. Tori is the regional alpha. She can give support. It's in all of their best interests."

I tried to keep up with their pack politics, but the only thing that rang in my head was Lana telling Callista and Kael to go. Which meant—

"I'll go with Destin. He can show me the site, and then once I know what the situation is, we can reconvene." Lana leaned back in her chair. She was trying hard not to look at me and didn't know that I could feel the spike in her heart rate. *Was she afraid of me?* I scowled.

"That okay by you?" Kael gave me a questioning glance.

"Do I have a choice?"

"No." Lana stood, drinking the last of her coffee and rinsing her mug with the pump at the sink.

After gathering their things, Kael and Callista said their goodbyes. Lana was still in the bathroom. When she reappeared, her hair was pulled back in a braid.

I'd packed the night before when I was restless. My pack was twice the size of hers, and she raised an eyebrow. I wanted to tell her she'd be grateful, but instead, I slung my pack over my shoulder without a word and stopped by the door.

Lana took the non-perishable food I'd set out on the table and stowed it in her bag, then stalked forward and put on her boots. She followed me out, and we started hiking up the trail in silence. The only sounds came from the crunch of our boots on the trail and the occasional rustle of leaves in the wind. I kept my eyes on the path ahead, trying to ignore the way my wolf was pacing inside me.

After nearly an hour, Lana broke the silence. "Are we going to walk the whole way?"

I glanced over at her, then back at the trail. "Where we're going, there aren't roads. And I have some errands to run."

"Errands?"

I nodded, not elaborating. She didn't need to know what I was doing or who I was seeing. She didn't need to know anything about me.

We reached the first cabin, a small, sturdy structure nestled in the forest. Smoke curled from the chimney, and sounds of life pulsed through the walls. My wolf settled as I approached the door and knocked. The latch lifted, and a she-wolf looked up at me with a relieved expression. "Destin, thank you for coming."

I nodded, then stepped inside, motioning for Lana to follow. "How's he doing, Ingrid?"

She stepped back and motioned to the main room, where a young wolf lay on a cot, his leg bandaged up to the knee. "Better, but I want to ensure the bone's set and there's no infection."

I crouched next to the boy and placed a hand on his shoulder. "Hey, bud. How's it feeling?" I'd received word the day before that he'd fallen out of a tree while I'd been gone. If Kael, Callista, and Lana hadn't shown up, I would've been here last night. Guilt settled in my gut that I hadn't been there to look after him the day it happened. Since wolves heal faster, setting a bone correctly and quickly was imperative.

He looked up at me with wide eyes, pain etched into his features. "It hurts, but I can move my toes now."

"That's good. I'm just going to take a look, okay?" He nodded, and I gently unwrapped the bandage. The skin around the wound was swollen and bruised, but there was no sign of infection.

Ingrid hovered behind me. "I told him a million times not to go up there, but he doesn't listen."

I nodded, then started re-wrapping the bandage. "You're a tough one, aren't you?" I smiled as the boy nodded. "This looks like it's healing well. Keep it elevated and try to stay off it as much as possible for the next couple of days." I looked up at Ingrid. "If the swelling doesn't start to go down or if it gets red and hot to the touch, let me know."

She nodded, and I stood, patting the boy on the shoulder. "You're going to be just fine. Running again by next week." As I turned to leave, I caught Lana's eye. She'd been standing silently in the corner, watching the whole interaction.

"Thank you, Destin. Truly." Ingrid stepped forward and grasped my hand, and I gave it a squeeze.

"Of course. If you need anything else, let me know." With a final nod, I walked out the door and back onto the trail.

Lana followed, her expression more subdued than it had been before. "You do that often?"

"Do what?" I hadn't done anything.

"Set bones. Treat patients." She glanced back at the cabin, then up at me.

"When I can."

She didn't respond, and we hiked again in silence until we reached the next cabin. I could tell immediately something was off. The air was thick with a scent I recognized all too well. My wolf stood at attention. *Shit.* I frowned and knocked on the door.

It creaked open, and a she-wolf with flushed cheeks and a sheen of sweat on her brow peered out. "Destin, thank you for coming." Her voice was strained, her breath coming in quick bursts. And then she turned and saw Lana. Immediately, her expression clouded over.

Annika was in heat. And she'd called for me.

I coughed. "What do you need help with, Annika?"

Annika stepped back, her eyes darting to Lana and then back to me. "The shutter on the back window broke, and I can't get it to stay up. I don't want to risk it falling in the middle of the night," she snapped. At least she had a real complaint. Save us both the embarrassment.

I nodded, then motioned for her to lead the way. As we walked around the side of the cabin, I could feel Lana's gaze burning a hole in my back. I crouched next to the broken shutter. "This won't take long." I pulled out my multi-tool from my pack and set to work, ignoring the way Annika's scent was making my stomach flip. I didn't want her. Not in the least. But that scent was meant to drive wolves wild. It was simple biology.

I worked quickly, securing the shutter and reinforcing the latch. "That should hold." I stood and brushed off my hands, then turned to Annika. Normally, I'd ask if there was anything else she needed, but by the way her lips flushed, I only took a step back.

Her eyes flicked to Lana, then to me again. "I'm making cottage pie this afternoon. If you have time to stop back." Her eyes bore into me. *Alone.*

I nodded, then started back toward the trail. Lana followed, her steps quick and purposeful. The silence felt thick. "Just say it."

Lana snorted. "Do you do *that* often?"

I didn't need to ask what she was referring to that time, and I didn't need to answer. The truth was, I was a rogue living alone in the middle of the woods. If a lone she-wolf needed me for more than fixing her shutter, I was usually happy to provide assistance.

I stopped and turned. Lana almost ran into me, and I dropped my head to stare down at her. "Do you have a mate?" I already knew the answer by her scent. By the loneliness that clung to her.

She swallowed hard. "No."

"Then how do you handle it?"

She opened her mouth, then snapped it closed. I turned and continued on through the forest. There. At least she knew I was more than open to a little stress relief if the mood hit her. My wolf was practically panting, and I walked faster. My breaths came in sharp, clipped puffs, and I flexed my fingers, the chill in the air doing little to soothe the heat simmering under my skin.

"Why do you do it?" Lana asked, and I almost laughed.

"Well, you see—"

"Not that," she growled. "Why do you help them? You don't want to be a part of a pack, and yet you act like—"

I whirled on her. "I'm not an alpha. I don't require their allegiance or obedience."

Lana's eyes narrowed. "What about their love and respect?"

I blew out a breath. "You've seen I'm very respectable."

She laughed as I turned and kept walking. "Ah. So that's it, then. You're paying penance for something."

I ground my teeth. She needed to stop talking.

"What do you think you did that required you to leave your pack and live the rest of your life doing good deeds?" I didn't answer, but Lana wouldn't let it go. "You and Kael. Your alphas really twisted your minds, didn't they?" She was breathing hard, taking long strides to keep up on the incline. "Packs are about family, support, loyalty."

A derisive snort escaped me. "Yeah, and with family comes expectations, obligations, and all the other shit I don't want to deal with."

"Because you don't want to screw up again?" Her voice dripped with sarcasm.

"Because I don't want to be responsible for anyone else." I spat the words, my chest tightening.

Lana reached out and grabbed onto my arm, pulling me to a stop. "You're not responsible for me, Destin. This is my choice."

I stared out through the trees. "Good to know."

~

WE ARRIVED at an abandoned hostel two hours later. The building was weathered, its wooden beams greyed with age and overgrown with moss. The hostel had been built for human hikers but had been left to rot decades ago. Even the closest small town was over twenty kilometers from here.

I set up a lantern since the sun was dropping. The wooden walls creaked in the wind as I dropped my pack and unloaded the simple food I'd brought. Sandwiches and dried meat. I pulled out a small propane heater and heated water in a metal canister.

"You're pretty responsible for someone who doesn't want to be." Lana watched me.

I grunted without looking up. Once the water was hot, I stepped outside and returned with a handful of herbs. I dropped them into the canister, and the air filled with the scent of chamomile and mint.

Lana took a mug gratefully, and we sat in silence, sipping the tea. The warmth spread through my chest. I watched the way Lana's hands wrapped around her cup, the way her eyes flickered in the dim light.

When heat beyond the tea began building in my middle, I stood and stretched, scanning to determine the best way to set up our mats. The only times I'd been here, I'd been alone. I walked to my pack and pulled out the tightly packed blankets.

"I have one. Not a mat, but a blanket." Lana reached for her bag.

I nodded and set the extra on the floor next to my bag. Then the light on the lantern flickered, and the hair on the back of my neck stood on end. I stilled, my eyes scanning the room.

"Did you hear that?" Lana whispered.

I nodded, my body tense. "Stay here." I pulled my knife from my bag and moved to the door. The night was still. I listened, straining to pick up anything out of the ordinary. Then it came again. Not a sound. A feeling.

I sucked in a breath as the door handle suddenly froze over.

NINE

LANA

The air turned cold and strange as Destin growled and released the door handle.

"What is it?" I reached for the dagger.

Destin stormed across the room and looked out the window. I followed, standing next to him. The night was a blanket of black, with the moon obscured behind the trees, but three dark silhouettes cut through the sky, their wings beating a thrumming rhythm that I felt deep in my chest.

"What the—?" Those were too big to be ravens or even eagles. My mind spun, searching for any kind of explanation.

Dark creatures. The last time I'd felt air like this was during the attack on Black Lake. I was only ten years old—

Glass shattered, and Destin rolled his body between me and the window. "Get down!" he growled, but I was sure as hell not going to hide while he fought off whatever was coming at us.

Destin spun as one of the dark creatures dove through the window, its talons outstretched. The other two were quick to follow and aimed at me. I crouched, ready to meet them, but those black wings were faster than I anticipated. A flash of movement from the corner of my eye, and I saw Destin grappling with the first bird, its talons raking at his face.

I growled, trying to focus. The dagger was in my hand, and suddenly, the pieces snapped into place. They knew it was there. Why else would they be attacking a random hostel in the middle of the woods? We were far from pack protection, and I had one of the most powerful items in the history of our world.

Stupid.

"Shrikes!" Destin growled.

Creatures from the legends we were told as kids. They existed?

I slashed at the closest one, but it swerved, its wings brushing past my cheeks. The other one darted in from the side, its beak aiming for my neck. I lowered my head, and it missed by a hair, its talons raking across my shoulder instead. Pain seared through my flesh, but I didn't have time to think about it.

Shadows obscured the light from the lantern. All I could hear was shrieking and the beat of feathers. I needed to shift. I should—

Sharp pain lanced across my arm, and I whirled, stabbing the blade through the air.

"I said, get down!" Destin shouted again, and I listened, but only for a second. My eyes adjusted, and I caught one of the shrikes off guard. It screeched, feathers flying, but the second one took advantage of my distraction. Its talons hooked into my side, and searing pain flashed through me as they dug deep.

I cried out, my vision blurring. I tried to shift, to force the transformation, but the blood was already pooling too fast. I couldn't focus. I couldn't breathe.

I staggered back, my legs trembling. I had to protect the dagger. I had to—

My limbs gave out, and I collapsed onto the sagging wooden floor. The world spun, and I fought to keep my eyes open, to stay conscious. Blood poured from my wounds, pooling around me, soaking my skin.

I heard a snarl, low and guttural, and my heart stuttered in my chest. Destin. He transformed through the haze, his muscles rippling and skin tearing. His fur was dark as midnight, his eyes glowing with a feral light.

He launched himself at the shrikes, his jaws snapping shut on one of their wings. Feathers exploded into the air, dark and shimmering in the moonlight. The shrike screeched, but it was cut off as Destin's teeth tore through its flesh, ripping it apart.

Blood sprayed, and I flinched as the droplets hit my skin, hot and sticky. The second shrike tried to flee, but Destin was faster. He lunged, his massive paws slamming into the bird's back, forcing it to the ground. His claws raked through its feathers, and with a final, bone-chilling snarl, he crushed its skull between his jaws.

The room fell silent. Destin stood over the mangled bodies, his chest heaving with exertion, his fur matted with blood. He shifted back to his human form without hesitation, his clothes shredded, all of him exposed. He didn't care. He didn't take the time to find something to cover himself. He dropped to his knees next to me, his hands immediately going to my middle. I felt pressure, then a searing heat as he pressed his palm to my skin. I tried to focus on his face, on the dark intensity of his eyes.

My vision tunneled, and the last thing I saw was the dark moon rising higher in the sky behind him through the shattered window. My body was numb, my mind foggy. I felt a warmth spreading from his touch, but I was bleeding too much, too fast.

Darkness closed in, and I fought against it, but my body was too weak. What had I told him? That he wasn't responsible for me? "Destin, I'm sorry—"

"Shut your mouth, Lana. Just close your eyes and breathe."

I woke, and my mouth felt like it had been swabbed with cotton balls. I blinked, taking stock of the darkness around me. It was still night. A low fire crackled next to me, sending sparks up into the air.

My midsection ached, but the pain was a dull throb compared to the searing agony I'd felt before. I adjusted my position on the floor, and that's when I noticed my shirt was gone. In its place, clean fabric was wrapped around me just beneath my bra, snug against my skin. It smelled like the forest, like leather, like—

"Destin?" My voice was a whisper, and I turned my head to see him sitting near the fire, his eyes reflecting the flames.

He nodded, his expression unreadable. "How are you feeling?"

I took a deep breath, wincing as my ribs protested. "Better than I should be."

Destin watched me, his eyes dark. "You were out for less than an hour. I wrapped your wound as best I could, but you were losing too much blood."

I nodded, my mind racing. The shrikes. Dark creatures. We hadn't seen any of them in over ten years. That was what our packs were for. To protect humans from their world being invaded by the darkness, but our packs hadn't heard a peep. Not a whisper.

I ran my fingers over the bandage and realized it was a shirt. A shirt that wasn't mine. I gripped the hem and tried to peel it up to see my wound.

"Don't." His voice was firm but not harsh. "It's still healing."

I frowned and was about to protest when I remembered the dagger. My heart skipped a beat, and I reached instinctively for my belt. It wasn't there.

My breath caught in my throat, and I sat up too quickly, the world tilting around me. "Where is it?" My voice was panicked, my vision narrowing.

Destin held up a hand, and I saw the glint of the dagger. My pulse pounded as he extended it to me. I snatched it from him and pressed it against my chest. "You—"

"It was covered in your blood." He motioned to the floor, and I saw my belt, the leather soaked through. Along with my pants and—

"Did you undress me?"

His brow furrowed. "I cleaned you up."

I bristled and looked down, finally taking stock of my state of undress. My heart skipped. I was in my underwear, and that was not the underwear I'd put on that morning. It was clean.

My mind whirled. Had he seen everything? Yes, he was saving my life, but still. My cheeks flamed, and I crossed my arms over my middle, even though I was covered by his damn shirt. "You could've waited until I woke up."

Destin scoffed. "Wait for you to freeze? Sure, that sounds like a great plan."

I glared at him. He leaned back, his expression unreadable. "I did what needed to be done. You were hurt, and I helped you. That's it."

I swallowed my pride. He was right. He'd taken care of me when I couldn't, and here I was snapping at him. "I'm sorry. Thank you."

Destin stared at the fire, and I found myself staring at the way the flickering light danced over his skin. He had a new shirt on. New pants. I pursed my lips at the brief flashes of him hovering over me after he'd shifted back.

I'd grown up with too many stories of men trying to take advantage of women in their vulnerable states. My mother had drilled it into me—never let your guard down. I remembered the first time I'd gone to a bar with a couple of friends from high school. I was wearing a tank top and shorts, nothing scandalous, but enough to get attention. A man from town made a move, tried to pull me onto his lap. I put him in the hospital.

"I don't like not knowing what happened," I whispered.

Destin turned his head. "If you think I'd do anything to hurt another wolf, you haven't been paying attention." He stood and walked back to his pack, then laid out his bed roll next to the fire. Far from the pool of my blood, still sticky on the floor. He laid out mine next to it, then took my blanket from the corner and tossed it over. He stood and rolled out his neck.

I scanned the room, noting that the only thing left of the shrikes were a few black feathers. There were already branches held in place over the broken window. "They wanted the dagger. I'm sure of it." That was the only thing that made sense. There was no reason for us to be a target.

Except for my blood.

Except for the relic.

I swallowed the lump in my throat. "Will we be safe here?"

Destin grunted as he lay down on his mat. He didn't have the answer. I shouldn't have even asked.

~

I woke with a start, blinking. The fire had burned down to glowing embers, casting faint shadows on the walls. For a moment, I couldn't remember where I was or why I was there. Then the memory of the night shrikes and the searing pain in my abdomen crashed over me.

I reached down and pulled up Destin's shirt to inspect the wound, expecting to find a gaping, bloody mess. Instead, I found smooth, unbroken skin. My breath caught in my throat. I'd felt the talons, the warmth of my blood spilling out of me.

I should've died.

It wasn't a dramatic statement. It was fact. Even with my shifter abilities, there was no way I should've healed that fast. I traced my fingers over where the wound had been, feeling the faint ridge of newly formed skin. It was still tender, and I winced as I pressed down.

There was a rustling outside, then the door to the hostel opened. Destin ducked inside, carrying something in his hands. He crouched next to me, and I caught a whiff of something earthy and herbal.

"Eat." He handed me a plate with some kind of meat and a bowl of steaming liquid that looked like pine needles had been boiled in water and then strained through someone's dirty socks.

I stared at it, then back at him. "What is this?"

"Food." He sat across from me, his eyes dark in the low light. The morning air clung to him.

I raised an eyebrow. "I can see that, but what's in it?"

Destin shrugged. "Meat and broth. It's good for you."

I hesitated, then took a tentative sip of the broth. It was surprisingly warm and soothing as it slid down my throat, spreading a gentle heat through my chest. The taste was strange, not unpleasant, but definitely not something I was used to. I took another sip, then a third, and before I knew it, the bowl was empty.

Destin watched, then reached out and took the bowl from my hands. He handed me the plate of meat. I tore into it, my hunger suddenly overwhelming.

Halfway through my meal, I got up and walked to my pack. I set the plate down and pulled out my phone. It was holding a charge, and I actually had a couple of bars of service. I tapped out a text to our group.

> Hey. We're on our way to the site. Just wanted to let you know I'm not dead.

Callista:

> Not dead, either. Almost back to Black Lake.

THAT MEANT they'd driven through the night again.

KAEL:

> Send us information when you get there.

> Will do. Keep me posted on Rowan and Evelyn.

I PUT my phone away and looked up at Destin. He was silent, watching me with those intense eyes. I reached down to the plate and ate the last bite of meat. "Thank you for this."

He nodded once. "Time to go."

CHAPTER
TEN

Destin

We shifted and ran most of the day. Lana's wolf was strong despite her ordeal. My limbs still ached from my own wounds, but by the time we stopped for the night at the last hostel on our route, I felt almost normal.

There were no attacks that night. The shrikes almost seemed like a fever dream. I woke on our second morning before dawn, the early morning light filtering through the forest canopy and casting dappled shadows on the walls. For a moment, I couldn't place where I was.

Then the smell of cooking meat pulled me fully awake, and I sat up, my eyes locking onto Lana at the stove.

"You're up." She didn't look over.

"You're making breakfast." It was a statement more than a

question. The scent of sizzling rabbit hit my nostrils. I was impressed. "You trapped that?"

"Yeah." She shrugged as if it was the most normal thing in the world.

"And you found the stove?" My voice was still thick with sleep, and I cleared my throat.

"I did." She turned, and her lips curved into a small smile. "I hope you don't mind, but I was freezing when I woke up. I searched a bit and found this."

I shook my head, trying to clear the fog. "No, it's fine. I just . . ." I looked at the camp stove. "You've used one before?"

Lana scoffed. "I'm not a princess. I have camped."

"I didn't mean—"

"You're not the only one who can be useful." She raised an eyebrow, then turned her attention back to the pan and flipped the rabbit leg with a stick.

My eyes fell to her stomach. Healed. My makeshift bandage was gone, and her skin was probably a smooth expanse . . .

A dull ache started in my chest, and I cleared my throat, forcing my gaze away. My wolf whined. "Sleep well?" I asked gruffly. Probably the stupidest question I'd ever asked. That was why I preferred to stay silent.

She nodded. "You?"

"Yeah." I lied. I'd slept for a solid five hours, but it wasn't restful. Not with my wolf on edge, sensing every shift in Lana's breathing, every movement of her body next to mine.

We sat in silence for a moment, the only sound the sizzle of the cooking rabbit. "I didn't want to wake you," she said finally, breaking the silence. "You seemed like you needed it."

I grunted in response.

"Here." Lana plated the rabbit and handed me half.

I took it without a word, biting into the tender meat. It was gamey but satisfying, and I couldn't help but feel a surge of gratitude. People didn't cook for me. People didn't do anything for me.

Then the reality of what we were doing cut through my momentary softening. Lana believed in the legends, the relics. She was actively trying to bring them back. I couldn't get on board with that. I'd spent my entire life trying to avoid the shifter games. The pack politics. My wolf had no interest in taking orders from anyone, and I had no interest in bending my will to another alpha. Even if her intentions were good, I knew how that kind of power would be taken advantage of. I'd watched it play out too many times to be hopeful.

Lana turned off the stove and disconnected the small propane tank. I fought the pull to watch her. My wolf was more attuned to her than I'd ever experienced with another wolf, and it was starting to piss me off. I was used to being in control of my instincts, but with her, it was a constant battle. Every time she was near, my senses were heightened to the point of distraction.

I could hear her heartbeat, smell the soap on her skin, feel the heat radiating from her body. It was intoxicating, and I hated that I was so affected.

It was only a product of our situation. I was starving. For connection, for touch, for something real. And Lana was the only thing in my immediate vicinity that satisfied those cravings.

It had to be that. If it wasn't, then I would have to face the fact that I was drawn to a wolf who believed in fairy tales and wanted to bring back relics that could potentially destroy our world.

I tore off a piece of meat with my teeth, chewing slowly as I watched her.

"Do you want more?" She turned to me, her eyes meeting mine for the first time since she'd woken up.

I shook my head, swallowing. "No, I'm good."

She nodded and took the last piece of rabbit for herself, sitting back against the wall as she ate. I watched her, my eyes tracing the curve of her neck, the way her hair fell over her shoulder.

When she finished, she set the plate down and stood, brushing off her hands. "We should get moving, right?"

I nodded, pushing to my feet.

We packed up in a few minutes and were back on the trail. The air was cold against my skin as we walked, the sun barely peeking over the horizon. I needed to show her the site. I needed to get this over with and get as far away from the relics and her as possible.

My wolf growled in protest, but I ignored him. I had a mission. A purpose. And it wasn't to chase after a she-wolf. Again, I wondered if she'd be up for a quick release. A moment to forget about the relics and the legends. Maybe she felt what I did, and we both needed to get it out of our systems. Having a night with Lana would erase my physical longing for her.

It had worked every other time.

"Time to shift." I dropped my pack.

Lana nodded and stepped into the trees so she could undress. When she was finished, I knelt and strapped her bag to her back, ensuring it wouldn't slip as she ran. She looked up at me, her amber eyes gleaming. Her gray coat was sleek and thick. She had a patch of white under her chin and at the tips of her ears. I refrained from petting her, knowing it would possibly get my hand taken off.

I stood and walked a few paces into the trees, then started stripping off my clothes, shoving them into my bag. I didn't worry about getting out of view. I should have, but a part of me wanted her to watch. Selfish, yes. I was owning it.

I loosened the straps of my bag as far as they would go and

gave in to my wolf. I'd done it enough times successfully without ripping my bag, and I hoped this wasn't the anomaly. The transformation was quick, and I felt the familiar rush of power as my senses heightened. The forest came alive around me—the rustle of leaves, the snap of twigs, the earthy scents.

Lana waited next to a cedar, and I stepped up beside her, my muscles coiled and ready for the run ahead. We took off, our paws pounding the ground in unison. The wind whipped through my fur, and Lana kept pace with me, her movements fluid and effortless.

We wove through the trees, leaping over fallen logs and ducking under low-hanging branches. Mid-morning, we stopped to hunt. I spotted a group of grouse pecking at the ground near a clearing, and we split up, circling around them silently. With a burst of speed, we lunged, our jaws snapping down on our prey.

The taste of warm blood filled my mouth, and I tore into the bird, devouring it in seconds. Lana did the same, her eyes gleaming with satisfaction. We didn't need to speak. Couldn't, since we weren't pack mates. But the hunt was in our blood, connecting us in a way that words never could.

After our meal, we continued north, the air growing colder with each passing minute. We paused to drink from a stream, the water icy and refreshing. With every step, the chill seeped deeper into my bones. The pads of my paws grew numb, and my breath puffed out in white clouds.

I led us into a clearing with fresh spring water trickling nearby. The sky above us was open and exposed. My wolf bristled at the vulnerability, and I immediately set to work. I couldn't control the space, but I could protect us from the wind and cold. I retreated to the tree line and started gathering branches and leaves.

I chopped a few large branches free with my hatchet, then

arranged the fallen limbs into a crude lean-to, bracing them against the trunks of the trees. I piled leaves and pine needles on top for insulation, creating a barrier against the elements. It wasn't much, but it would do.

Next, I searched for tinder and kindling, picking up dry twigs and dead grass. Lana jumped in to help. When we had enough, I positioned the materials in a small depression I'd dug out with my hands, then pulled out my flint and steel from my pack. With a few strikes, sparks flew, and a small flame flickered to life. I fed it slowly, adding larger sticks until the fire crackled and danced.

I cleared my throat as I stood, brushing the dirt and needles from my hands. "This should be enough to get us through the night."

Lana nodded. "It's good. I wouldn't have thought to make a shelter."

I sat on the ground next to the fire. "You learned this stuff when you went camping?"

"More or less."

I waited, wondering if she'd say more. She stepped closer to the fire, holding her hands out to the warmth. I was rewarded for my patience when she blew out a breath and continued.

"When I was sixteen, my dad dropped me and my brother in the woods with nothing but the clothes on our backs. Told us to find our way home."

I blinked. "Intense."

Lana shrugged. "It was. He'd given us some practice beforehand. But it was different relying on myself."

I nodded. "And he taught you to fight?"

She wet her lips. "I've been training in Krav Maga since I was twelve."

I raised an eyebrow. "Krav Maga?"

She smiled, the firelight glinting off her eyes. "Self-defense."

I swallowed hard, ignoring how my pulse quickened at the thought of her getting fired up and fighting. I hadn't seen more than a blur of shadow and feathers in the hostel. "Sounds like you're more than capable of handling yourself, then."

Lana's smile faded, and she looked back at the fire. Sorrow and maybe a little anxiety filtered over from her, and I instantly wanted to lift her spirits.

I blew out a breath. "Do you want to spar?"

Lana's eyes flicked to mine. "Now?"

"Yeah, it's a good way to warm up before bed. Unless you want to freeze your ass off tonight." I wasn't sure what had possessed me to suggest it, but I didn't regret it.

Her lips twitched, and she stood, brushing off her pants. "Alright then. But don't cry when I win."

I rolled my eyes. "Let's see what you've got. Princess."

Lana stepped back, and the two of us circled each other. I kept my stance loose, my hands up. She moved like a dancer, her footwork precise and fluid. I threw a few jabs, testing her, and she blocked them with ease. When she countered, I barely had time to react, her fist grazing my ribs.

I grinned. "Not bad."

"Not bad?" She feigned a look of shock.

I shrugged. "I just wanted to see how long it would take you to get a hit in."

Lana's eyes narrowed, and she lunged. I blocked her punch, then ducked under her arm, spinning her around. Her back pressed against my chest, and I was hyper-aware of the heat of her body against mine. My wolf growled, and I released her too quickly, stumbling back.

She turned, her eyes blazing. "You're holding back."

I raised an eyebrow. "You want me to go all out? I've got at least thirty kilos on you."

Lana nodded, her breath coming in quick pants. "What's the point if you don't?"

I hesitated but then nodded. I shifted my weight, and this time when I lunged, I didn't hold back. My fist connected with her forearm, and she winced, but she didn't back down. She countered with a series of quick jabs, and I had to move fast to block them.

Lana was quick, but I was stronger. I grabbed her wrist, twisting her arm behind her back. She grunted, then dropped to one knee, using her momentum to flip me over her shoulder. I landed hard on my back, the air whooshing out of my lungs.

I blinked up at her, stunned, and she grinned down at me. "The more force you put into it, the more I can use against you."

I chuckled, then reached up and grabbed her hand, pulling her down on top of me. She gasped as she landed on my chest, and for a moment, we were both still, our breaths mingling in the cold night air.

I wanted to kiss her. Hell, I wanted to do more than that, but I couldn't push. Not when I didn't know if she wanted it, too.

Lana's cheeks flushed, and she scrambled to her feet. "I think I'm warm enough now."

I nodded, pushing myself up. "Mmm."

We sat by the fire, eating the dried meat and nuts we'd packed. The food was simple, but it filled the gnawing emptiness in my stomach. As the fire died down, the cold crept back in, beginning to seep through my clothes. Time to get under our blankets before it was too late.

I stood and walked to our makeshift shelter, ducking under

the branches. Lana followed, and we rolled out our mats, then lay down on the pine needles, our bodies just inches apart.

I stared out at the dark sky, the branches above us swaying in the wind. My mind was a whirlwind of thoughts, but one kept surfacing over and over. I clenched my jaw, forcing myself to relax. Lana's breathing slowed, and I finally allowed myself to drift into the darkness.

I slept like a rock until a sound pulled me back to consciousness. It was faint but persistent. A shuffling, fabric against fabric. I opened my eyes, and my breath hitched. Lana was still next to me, her back turned.

I frowned, my brain still foggy from sleep. I reached out, my hand hovering just above her shoulder. She was shivering. The air was cold. Biting. But it didn't affect me the same way. I had more body mass, and whatever else made men heaters and women ice cubes.

I couldn't just lie there and do nothing. My wolf growled, and before I could second-guess myself, I closed the distance between us. I slid my arm under her head, pulling her against my chest.

Lana tensed, and I felt her breath hitch. "Destin, what are you doing?" Her voice was barely a whisper, sending a shiver down my spine.

I swallowed hard. "You're shivering."

"I can take care of myself."

Her ears were ice cold against my arm. "I'm cold," I lied, hoping she couldn't hear the thundering of my heart.

She was silent for a moment. Then she let out a soft breath. "Fine. If it helps you sleep."

I lay on my side, my arm wrapped over her hip, my body pressed against hers. I felt the contours of her form through the thin fabric of our clothes. Her scent was intoxicating. I inhaled deeply, my pulse quickening.

Lana adjusted, and her socked feet slid up between my calves. She sighed as my warmth spread through her, and I stifled a groan. I closed my eyes, trying to keep my hips back far enough that she wouldn't feel what was happening below the waistband of my pants.

I exhaled, and my lips brushed the shell of her ear. Her heartbeat quickened. Her emotions spiked. She wanted me. Even without my psi abilities, I could sense it in the way her body responded, in the way her breathing hitched every time I moved.

My wolf growled, urging me to press. But I couldn't. Not without her explicit consent. No matter how badly I wanted her, I wouldn't cross that line.

The tension in her muscles, the way she was holding herself back, drove me mad. I waited for her to do something, anything, but she only curled deeper into herself.

My wolf clawed at my insides. This was torture. Holding her like this, knowing I couldn't do anything about it. I wanted to run my hands over every inch of her body, to taste her skin, to hear her moan my name. Then, when I dropped her off at the site in the morning, I wouldn't have to think about her. To imagine her scent every damn day.

My annoyance grew with every breath she took. Every second that passed without her turning toward me. I was pissed that my wolf was in a frenzy for her. I was a rogue shifter. I lived in the wild and didn't answer to anyone. And here I was, lying next to a she-wolf with her feet between my legs. I was getting whipped before I'd even had a taste, and my wolf was all in on it.

Then I was pissed that she wouldn't put me out of my misery. It wasn't her fault, but it was late. My blood wasn't circulating properly in my head, and I had to blame someone.

I finally closed my eyes and accepted my fate. I was going to lie there with my balls in a vice grip.

At least Lana had stopped shivering.

CHAPTER
ELEVEN

I woke to warmth and weight. A heavy arm draped over my waist, and the solid wall of a body pressed against my back. I sucked in a breath, my heart hammering in my chest. Everything inside me stilled. I'd slept like a baby. In his arms. All night long.

My skin tingled where Destin's arm touched me, but it wasn't just that. The night before flung itself back into my memory, and my body was keenly aware of the place where his lips had accidentally brushed against my skin the night before. How he'd pulled his hips away from me, his breath heavy against my neck.

My wolf stirred, restless. *You're too stubborn for your own good.*

My eyes widened. *This? This is the moment you decide to talk to me again? You've been silent for days.*

I was giving you time.

I almost laughed out loud. *Time for what?* I moved my hips, trying to extricate myself without waking Destin, but it was like trying to move out from under a boulder. My movement only made things worse. His arm tightened around me, pulling me back against him. I froze as his body pressed even closer, and I was suddenly very aware of every muscle, every inch of him. The way his hips were now very much pressed against my backside.

My heart stuttered, and blood rushed in my ears.

He's strong. He's capable. My wolf started listing off all the qualities she'd found in Destin. Apparently she'd been watching in her silence.

He's a rogue, I hissed back.

Destin's arm tensed, then relaxed as he blinked awake. "Morning," he grumbled, his voice thick with sleep.

I turned my head. "Morning? Is that what we're calling this? Because it feels more like a hostage situation."

His lips curved into a lazy smile, and he didn't move his arm. "You complaining?"

"Maybe I am." I tried to sound indignant, but it came out breathy. Damn it.

He chuckled, a low, rumbling sound that vibrated against my back. "You're not complaining."

I swallowed hard. "Don't tell me what I am and am not doing."

"Fine, princess. But if you're going to keep moving like that, I'm going to start thinking you want something."

My cheeks flushed, and I shoved his arm off me, rolling away. "You're—" I couldn't find a word to finish that sentence because I suddenly realized his scent was all over me.

Destin stretched, and the hem of his shirt rode up,

exposing a sliver of skin. I looked away, focusing on the trees swaying in the morning breeze. "We should get moving."

Destin sat up, rubbing the back of his neck. "Yeah. Last leg. We'll be there this afternoon."

My shoulders tensed. "Perfect."

Are you going to miss him? My wolf sounded smug.

I stalked away from our camp and turned to the stream to find a place where I was mostly hidden. I was desperate to wash myself as best I could. Peeling off my jacket, I kicked off my boots and yanked my shirt over my head. The breeze scraped across my bare arms, and a shiver rippled through me, goosebumps rising in its wake. It wasn't just the cold—everything from the night still clung to me. Sweat, remnants of dried blood, and most troubling, *Destin*.

His scent stuck to me, earthy and wild, like it had stained my skin. Every breath stirred it back up, winding through my senses, making my pulse quicken in ways I refused to acknowledge. My hands fumbled at the waistband of my pants, shoving them down and kicking them off so I could wade into the stream. The water hit like ice, stabbing into my legs, sharp enough to steal the air from my lungs. I gritted my teeth and splashed it over my arms and chest, the cold jolting me awake.

I scrubbed harder, determined to wash away the salt, the blood, and every reminder of him. Without soap, his scent lingered. I splashed more water on my neck, letting it drip down my back, trying to drown the pull he had on me. But it wouldn't go away, not fully. And the worst realization? Some part of me didn't want it gone at all.

But he would be. In a matter of hours. And that was for the best. He could go on with his quiet life as he wanted, and I could . . . do whatever I was going to have to do next.

That thought sobered me, and the loneliness rushed back in.

I dressed, then the two of us packed up our gear in silence, the tension between us thick enough to cut with a knife.

"Ready?" I asked, my voice clipped.

Destin grunted in response, and we fell into our routine. We took turns shifting, and all the emotions swirling within me intensified. *Please don't do anything stupid*, I muttered.

Me? Never. I couldn't see it, but I could feel my wolf's mischievous grin. I gasped as she trotted up to Destin and stroked our entire body against his sleek, black coat. He let out a guttural yip, and my wolf danced ahead of him.

What the hell?

Whoops.

I could hear him panting behind us, and we'd barely taken a few steps. Thankfully my wolf was satisfied and began to run, the forest blurring around us. I tried to focus on the task at hand, not the fact that Destin was staring at our ass. We had a long day ahead of us, and I needed to be at my best.

After a few hours, Destin barked, and we pulled to a stop. He was hesitant, sniffing the area carefully before leading me forward. We walked through a slot canyon, then emerged in an open space between the rock faces. *One way in and one way out.*

Destin turned so I could shift and dress, then he did the same. When we were settled, he led me closer to the rock wall ahead of us. We were back below the tree line, and the mountain clearing was ringed with towering pines. The ground was a mix of rock and sparse vegetation, the air crisp and biting.

Then I saw it. A stone protruding from the ground, its surface unnaturally smooth. It wasn't a boulder or a slab of rock like the others. It was shaped, almost like it had been carved by hand, slate gray, and speckled with darker flecks.

Destin stayed back, his body tense. He wouldn't come any closer to the stone, and the look on his face was a mix of determination and . . . fear? It was the first time I'd seen him so skittish.

"This is it?" I asked, my voice hushed.

He nodded, his eyes fixed on the stone.

I took a step closer, my boots crunching on the cracking slate. "Looks like a rock to me."

Destin's jaw clenched, and a muscle twitched in his cheek. "It's not just a rock."

I nodded. "How do you know this place?"

He didn't answer.

I took another step closer, my curiosity piqued. He sucked in a breath and held it as I stopped in front of the stone. "You've done your job. You can go. I'll figure it out from here."

He didn't move, and somehow, I knew he wouldn't. He'd led me here, and as much as he played it tough, he wasn't about to leave me alone in the middle of the mountains. But part of me wished he would.

I felt self-conscious as I leaned down, inspecting the base of the stone. There were no markings, no inscriptions. Nothing to indicate that it was anything other than a chunk of rock. I stood up and dusted off my hands, turning to face him. "I don't have any traps handy. Can you please just tell me what you know?"

His eyes flicked to mine, and for a moment, I thought he was going to say something. Instead, he just stood there, silent and brooding.

I huffed and walked back over to the stone, determined to figure it out. If he wasn't going to be helpful, then I'd do it myself. I reached out and placed my hand on the stone, feeling the cool surface under my palm.

Destin flinched. "It needs blood, Lana."

I swallowed hard, placing my hand on the dagger. "How do you know that?"

Destin's gaze flickered, his eyes darting between mine and the stone. His lips parted as if he was about to speak, but then he hesitated, his jaw clenching. His hands curled at his sides, the tendons in his forearms standing out against the skin. Then his eyes darkened, and he lowered into a crouch so fast, I didn't have time to react. The next second, he was a blur, launching himself directly at me.

CHAPTER
TWELVE

The world shifted. Not physically, but emotionally. The air hummed with a sudden tension, a ripple of wrongness. Lana had just asked me a question, but I couldn't focus. There was no scent, no rustle in the leaves. Just the gnawing pull of instincts that had kept me alive for years. Something was coming. I knew it like I knew my own heartbeat.

The sensation peaked in front of me, and I crouched, launching myself toward Lana. Her head whipped around, eyes wide with shock, but before she could move, I was airborne. My body twisted mid-leap, bones snapping, sinew reshaping in a blur of heat and motion. My clothes shredded, left behind as my paws hit the ground with a thud.

The fur along my spine bristled as I collided with something that slipped out of the shadows like a nightmare made real. Gaunt and skeletal, its bone-white skin stretched tight over impossibly long limbs. Its eyes burned a sickly red, glowing with hunger, and its mouth opened in a silent, snarling grin.

A bone stalker. The kind of creature you heard about as a pup, tucked in by the fire, tales spun to keep you close to the den and out of the woods. I used to think those stories were bullshit. Just something the old wolves made up to scare us.

Until I'd seen one in the woods for myself.

I slashed at its chest with my claws, but the thing didn't bleed. It moved like a broken puppet—fluid and wrong all at once, its joints creaking as it twisted out of reach. I snapped my jaws at its neck, but it jerked away, limbs bending at angles that shouldn't exist.

Where the hell had this thing come from? My mind raced even as my instincts kept me moving, dodging and striking, but it was relentless. The damn thing moved like water, fluid and silent, slipping between my attacks without a pause. No hesitation. No pain. Just endless hunger.

I couldn't tell Lana to get out of there. Couldn't do anything but keep the stalker at bay. *Fire.* That was all I could remember about my research back then. Fire could kill them. Not helpful in the least.

The creature lunged again, and this time, I was ready. I shifted my weight at the last second, slamming my shoulder hard into its ribs. The brittle creak of bone reverberated through my chest, and the thing staggered back a step but didn't fall. Damn it.

I flicked my gaze toward Lana. She was scrambling in the dirt, her hands reaching for the dagger. After the incident with the birds from hell, Lana was sure she understood what these creatures were after, and I couldn't argue. But to protect the dagger, she couldn't shift. She couldn't protect herself.

A growl rumbled low in my throat. No way in hell was I letting this thing get anywhere near her. With a savage snarl, I launched myself at the Bone Stalker, claws gleaming under the thin sliver of moonlight that slipped through the trees.

Lana clenched the dagger, her knuckles white, and then another bone stalker burst into the clearing. It moved with the same eerie silence, its eyes locked onto her. It swayed back and forth, its bony limbs twitching, then lunged. Lana's reflexes kicked in, and she pivoted on her heel, bringing the dagger up just in time. The blade sank into the creature's side, and for a split second, it seemed to hang in midair. Then it howled, a sound that was more vibration than noise, and recoiled just as my stalker attacked again.

We weren't going to win this fight. Not with Lana forced to stay in human form. She could spar, but not with creatures like this. I wouldn't chance a fight without my wolf.

I had to get a message to her. As terrified as I was about what would happen with the stone, she needed to activate it. If the ground tried to swallow us up like it had the last time I was here, so be it. Maybe it would take the bone stalkers with us.

My jaws clamped around the first bone stalker's throat as it tore toward my belly. I shook it like a rag doll, and tossed it toward the rock face. With a sickening crunch, the creature went limp. It wouldn't last long.

I bolted toward Lana, knocking the stalker back, then growling and tossing my head toward the stone.

Lana understood instantly. She didn't hesitate, just dragged the dagger over her palm, wincing as the blade bit into her skin. Blood welled up, and she smeared it across the surface of the stone.

The second stalker was on me, and the first was lifting to its feet. I fought. My jaws snapped, but I was tiring fast.

At first, nothing happened, but then the stone began to pulse with a soft, inner light. The air around us grew thick and heavy, like the atmosphere before a storm.

The bone stalker growled, lashing out, its movements jerky and desperate. Something was happening. It lunged with ferocity toward Lana, and I threw my body in front of it as the light from the stone grew brighter, tendrils of light beginning to curl and twist, reaching out like living things.

I didn't have time to admire it. I lunged, crashing into the bone stalker on my left. The creature screeched, its bony claws scraping against my fur, but I didn't back down. *He was not getting to Lana.*

Then pure energy surged through me. The bone stalkers screeched in unison, their chalk-white forms blurring as they lunged. But it was too late. Lana's hand was on my back, and I was being dragged back toward her.

My vision blurred, the air around me thickening like I was falling through honey. Darkness swirled, punctuated by flashes of light. This was it. We were being swallowed up.

But it felt nothing like the first time. The ground wasn't shaking, instead it seemed to disappear entirely. My stomach lurched as if I were plummeting off a cliff. I wanted to cry out, to search for Lana, but even the sound of my breath was swallowed by the void. There was nothing but the rush of air and the strange, otherworldly glow.

Then, as suddenly as it began, it was over. My feet hit solid ground. *Feet, not paws.* The world snapped into focus, and I blinked, my eyes adjusting.

Everything was quiet. Too quiet. I spun, my heart still racing, and realized we were no longer in the clearing. Or at least, not in the same clearing. The trees around us were the same, but there was a quality to the air, a softness to the light that made everything seem ethereal. Like we were in a dream.

"What is this place?" Lana's voice was a whisper.

I whirled to face her. We were both human again, but not the same. Lana wore a dress that looked like it belonged in a museum. The fabric was soft and flowing, with intricate lace detailing. A corset cinched her waist, and the sleeves puffed out at her shoulders before tapering down to her wrists. It was beautiful, but by the scowl on her face, she wasn't a fan.

I couldn't blame her. It was completely impractical. I glanced down and saw I was magically clothed. I wore a waist-coat over a crisp white shirt, with dark trousers and polished boots. I frowned, running a hand through my hair. "This is . . . I don't know what this is."

This was insane. It had to be some kind of hallucination. Maybe we'd hit our heads on the way down. We were dead and didn't even know it.

We turned as one to look at the stone, and I sucked in a breath. The bone stalkers were still there, their skeletal forms prowling the clearing. But they seemed . . . confused. They sniffed the air, their glowing eyes scanning the area, but they didn't seem to notice us standing there.

It was like we were in a different dimension, watching a scene play out in front of us. My heart pounded in my chest.

What had we done?

Lana's eyes widened. "Destin, look."

I turned to where she was pointing. A bright light, glowing in the distance. It was the only thing in this strange, ethereal landscape that seemed solid. Real.

I took a step forward, and Lana followed. The bone stalkers continued their search, oblivious to our movement. As we approached the light, I felt a pull, like a magnet drawing us in.

Lana reached for my hand, and I laced my fingers through hers.

"I'm sorry," she murmured. "I didn't—you were supposed to leave. I don't know what this is, Destin. Maybe you can—"

"I'm going with you."

She looked up at me, her eyes wary. "You're not responsible for me, remember?"

That was bullshit. And we both knew it.

CHAPTER
THIRTEEN

Lana

Selfishly, I couldn't have been happier that Destin was by my side. I felt safe with him. Even though neither of us knew what we were walking toward, it was a relief not to be alone.

We moved together, our steps careful and deliberate. The light seemed to beckon us, and I couldn't resist its pull.

As we approached, the shadows around us thickened, and the air vibrated. The hairs on the backs of my arms lifted.

Then, in a burst of blinding radiance, the light expanded, and I felt a presence. It wasn't anything I could make out with my physical senses, but it was there.

"I don't like this," Destin murmured.

My thoughts exactly. My wolf prowled, so on edge she couldn't form words.

Without warning, the presence spoke. *Welcome, daughter of*

the Shadow Pack. It wasn't a voice in the traditional sense. It was more like a thought, a feeling that resonated deep within my bones. I shivered, the sensation both exhilarating and terrifying.

Destin bared his teeth. I didn't know what to say or how to respond.

The light shifted, its glow taking on a different hue. As if it were . . . aware. I held my breath as the presence wrapped around me again, and I felt words as if they were being pulled from my own thoughts. *You possess one of the relics.*

My heart skipped a beat. How had it known? I hadn't said anything about the dagger. I hadn't even thought about it. The light pulsed. *The relics are not easily found. They are meant for those who are worthy.*

Worthy. I almost snorted. The alphas were anything but, and yet they had found the dagger. "What does that mean?"

The presence seemed to swirl around me, its energy like a river flowing through my veins. *Worthy of their power. Worthy of their cost.*

I frowned. "Cost?"

The presence withdrew slightly, and I felt a chill in its absence. *You have questions.* The presence rushed back in, its energy ebbing and flowing like a tide.

I nodded, even though I wasn't sure it could see me. "Yes. I . . . I was looking for something. A relic."

The air around us seemed to hum with anticipation. *The relics are not easily found.*

I swallowed hard. "I know. But I have to try. My pack—"

Your pack is in danger. The presence finished my sentence, and a cold dread settled in my stomach.

"Yes." I took a deep breath, trying to steady myself. Not just my pack. All the packs. But what hit me the hardest was that this being had recognized that I still had one to belong to. The light pulsed, and I felt a pressure in my chest, like a hand pressing down on my heart. *You seek the Book of Shadows.*

I nodded again. So, it had a name. "Yes. Where can I find it?"

The presence seemed to hesitate, and then I felt a wave of something wash over me. It wasn't quite emotion, not anger or frustration, but it was close. *The Book of Shadows is not for the faint of heart. It requires a sacrifice.*

My heartbeat pounded in my ears. "What kind of sacrifice?"

The presence didn't answer immediately, and a cold sweat broke out on my skin. My wolf paced. Destin gripped my hand tighter in his.

Finally, it spoke again. *The Book requires a test. A challenge of worthiness.*

The adrenaline rushing through my veins was making me jittery. "What kind of challenge?" I asked, my voice barely more than a whisper.

The presence seemed to shift, its light dimming slightly. *That is not for me to decide. But know this, daughter. The relics are not to be taken lightly. They carry great power, but also great danger.*

I nodded, my throat tight. "I understand." How was I going to explain this to Callista and Kael? I still wasn't convinced we hadn't died in the jaws of the bone stalkers.

The light pulsed again, and the pressure in my chest lessened. *You have made it this far. The path will not be easy, but it is yours to walk.*

I opened my mouth to ask another question, but before I could speak, the light began to fade. The presence withdrew, and the world around us started to shift back to the forest we'd left behind.

"Wait!" I called out, but it was too late. The light winked

out, leaving me and Destin alone in the moonlit clearing. Why hadn't I asked more about how we ended up here in the first place? *What this place was?*

I stood there, my heart racing, my mind spinning. What the hell just happened? I turned to Destin, who was still watching the spot where the light had been. "Did you—"

He nodded, his jaw clenched. "Yeah. I heard it." His shoulders were tense.

I took a step back, trying to give him space to process. To breathe. I reached out and touched one of the trees. My hand passed through it like it was made of smoke. I hissed, yanking my hand back. I tried again, this time with the ground. Same result. It was like there was a veil over everything, separating us from the real world.

I stood up, my hands trembling. "This doesn't make any sense."

Destin's jaw clenched. "Yeah."

I let out a shaky breath. "What do you think it meant by a challenge?" Destin didn't answer, and I stared at the spot where the light had been. "I'm sorry," I whispered.

"About what?"

"I don't know how to get you out of here, and—"

The light flared in front of us, and I jumped. *You will not leave until you have completed the challenge.* The words echoed in my mind, and I took a step back. Perfect. A nice ultimatum in the underworld.

There is no retreat. The path is set.

"Really hammering that home," I muttered. How long would this challenge take? What would it be? Kael and Callista were hopefully tracking the alphas by now, and we needed to be able to communicate with them.

The light flickered, and I felt a shift in its presence. It was as if it had noticed something for the first time. I didn't know how, but I felt the being's attention had turned to Destin. *He should not be here. He is not a son of the Shadow Pack.*

My grip tightened as fear flared through my midsection. Would he be forced to leave? Moments ago, I wanted to help him escape—to get back to his quiet home in the mountains. But now the idea of being alone in this gauzy reality made me want to throw up.

"I'm staying." Destin's voice was rough.

The presence seemed to hesitate, then withdrew slightly. *This is not wise.*

"No shit," Destin said on an exhale, and without warning, the ground and images around us began to transform.

My clothes changed from that ancient dress to battle garb. At least there was that.

The sky darkened, the trees disappeared, and in a snap, I stood at the entrance of a maze, my chest tightening as I took in the towering hedges that stretched up into the darkness. They looked like they were made of shadows, shifting and writhing as if they were alive. The path ahead was narrow, barely wide enough for me to squeeze through. I turned to Destin, but found the space next to me empty.

"Lana!" he called, and my head snapped up. There he was. Above me, standing at the edge of a cliff, on top of the rock face we'd found protecting the stone.

The light's words echoed in my mind. *Prove you're worthy.* This had to be it, then. My challenge. My heart pounded as I took a step forward, then another. The ground was uneven, rocks and roots jutting up to trip me at every turn.

"I'm watching. You can't see me, but I can see you," Destin shouted.

Okay. I clenched and unclenched my fists. I wasn't alone. I moved forward, the maze walls closing in around me. The air felt colder here, the shadows deeper. As I rounded the first corner, the path split into three separate directions. My pulse quickened. Great. A choose-your-own-adventure death trap.

A little help here? I pushed to my wolf. She surged forward, sniffing the air. Then I heard it—soft at first, but unmistakable. A low, guttural howl that crawled down my spine, followed by the slow, deliberate crack of bones realigning. My stomach knotted as recognition hit me. Bone stalker.

My wolf growled, working to catch the thing's scent, but there was nothing. No trace of it in the air, no sign in the soil. Just emptiness where a scent should be. A wave of unease washed over me—there was no hunting something that left no scent trail.

I spun, scanning the shadows pressing in on me. The maze twisted and morphed as if it knew what hunted me, as if it wanted to play along. A cold sweat broke out across my skin.

"Destin!" I shouted, trying to keep my voice steady. "I need you! I think there's a bone stalker in here."

I caught the briefest pause in his voice, like he'd been hit by the same fear I was barely keeping at bay. "Lana, stay calm. I see you. Just keep moving forward. Don't stop."

"Not helpful!" I hissed, my nails digging into my palms as I forced myself to take another step. The path narrowed further, the shadows writhing like they wanted to wrap around me. My wolf clawed at my mind, ready to fight but uncertain without a scent to guide her.

"Destin, can you see the maze? I need to know where this thing is."

"Yeah, I've got eyes on it from here. There's a clearing up ahead—go left at the next split."

A howl echoed again, closer this time, low and haunting. The sound turned my blood to ice. I needed to keep moving, needed to trust Destin's directions, even though every part of me wanted to bolt the other way.

The path split again, three different directions opening in front of me. My instincts screamed at me to choose, to run blindly, but I clenched my fists tighter and forced my wolf to calm. She whined in frustration, pacing in my mind.

"Which way, Destin?" My voice was sharp.

"Left," he answered quickly, his tone solid and grounding. "Go now."

I took off down the left path, the jagged ground threatening to trip me with every step. Behind me, the sound of bones cracking again—louder this time, closer. I pushed harder, my heart hammering in my chest.

I turned and ran straight into a hedge thrusting up from the ground. It was changing in real time. Creating new paths and closing off old ones.

A branch scraped against my cheek, and I winced as it drew blood. I didn't have time to think about the pain. I turned back and found a steep incline ahead. The path was barely wide enough for my feet, and the sides of the maze loomed on either side, making it feel like I was climbing through a tunnel.

I started up, my legs burning with the effort. The creature's growls were louder now, echoing off the walls. Its claws scraped against the ground. Faster. I needed to go faster.

"You're almost there!" Destin's voice was farther away now.

I reached the top of the incline and stumbled onto a flat section of path. My lungs were on fire, and I had to bend over, hands on my knees, to catch my breath. It was then I heard it. A rustling in the hedges.

I whipped around, my eyes scanning the shadows. The path was empty, but I could feel it. The creature was close. My instincts screamed at me to run, but I couldn't move. I was frozen, my muscles locked in place.

Almost where? The maze twisted around me, and just as I

felt the shadows press closer, my wolf surged forward, forcing me up. I scrambled to my feet and bolted. My lungs burned from the sprint, but I kept moving.

The howl came again, so close it felt like it was breathing down my neck. I spun toward the sound, teeth bared. My wolf surged, but something felt wrong. I knew with startling clarity that I wouldn't be able to shift here.

"Lana!" Destin's voice was sharp, and I forced myself to look up. I could barely see him now that I was higher up. He was pointing to my right. I turned just as the creature lunged from the hedge.

It was a blur of bones, rot, and teeth, and I barely had time to react. I threw myself to the side, hitting the ground hard. The creature skidded past me, its claws tearing up the earth.

I scrambled to my feet, my heart hammering in my chest. The creature turned, its eyes glowing red in the darkness. It was massive, easily twice the size of any wolf I'd ever seen. What fur it had was matted and slick with blood, and its teeth were bared in a snarl.

I took a step back, my mind racing. There was no way I could fight this thing. It was too fast, too strong. I had to outsmart it. The bone stalker lunged, and I dodged to the left. It crashed into the hedge, snarling in frustration. I took off down the path, my legs pumping. I had to find a way out.

The path opened up again, and I found myself standing on the edge of a chasm. A rickety bridge spanned the gap, the planks creaking and swaying in the wind. I hesitated, my heart pounding in my ears.

"There's no other way," Destin called from above. "You have to cross."

I nodded, my throat dry. I stepped onto the first plank, and it groaned under my weight. The darkness below seemed to stretch on forever—I couldn't see the bottom. I gripped the rope handrails, my knuckles turning white, and took another step. Then another.

The bridge swayed, and I had to fight to keep my balance. The wind whipped through the chasm, and I felt like I was walking on a tightrope. My muscles screamed in protest, but I kept moving.

I'd barely made it halfway when the bridge swung to my left. The bone stalker. It was there behind me. The planks under my feet started to break away. One by one, they snapped and fell into the abyss as I stumbled forward. My breath caught in my throat, and I quickened my pace.

"Run!" Destin's voice was urgent, and I didn't need to be told twice. I darted forward, the bridge buckling under my feet. The last plank snapped, and I leaped for the edge.

My fingers scraped against the dirt, and I grappled for a hold. My feet dangled over the edge, and I kicked, trying to find purchase. Finally, I managed to pull myself up.

I lay on my back, gasping for air. The bridge was gone, the planks and ropes scattered in the darkness below. I rolled over and pushed myself to my feet, my legs trembling.

"Lana, the walls are shifting!" Destin's voice was frantic, and I looked up. The walls of the maze were moving, closing in on me. I had to move fast.

I sprinted down the path, my eyes scanning for an exit. The walls were closing in, and I had to duck and weave to avoid getting crushed. My lungs ached, and my muscles felt like they were on fire, but I didn't stop.

Finally, I saw an opening. I dove through, hitting the ground hard. The walls slammed shut behind me, and I rolled to my knees, panting.

My head spun. I scanned the area around me just waiting for the bone stalker to throw itself from the hedge.

"Lana!" Destin's voice was filled with relief, and I looked up to see him running toward me now that we were on equal planes. He dropped to his knees next to me, his hands on my shoulders. "Are you okay?"

I nodded, unable to speak. My body was trembling, but I forced myself to my feet. I'd done it. With Destin's help, I'd made it through the maze.

I searched the air for the ghostly light, waiting for some sort of acknowledgment and hopefully the book.

Nothing came.

Instead, the maze shrank away, leaving us standing back in the ethereal woods. Instead of a bright light, a table appeared. My breath caught in my throat as I saw what lay on top of it.

CHAPTER

FOURTEEN

DESTIN

I moved closer to the table. Lana followed, her eyes fixed on the spread laid out before us. It was a thing of beauty, dark wood polished to a mirror finish. It stood in stark contrast to the haze around us, and the *food*.

The feast stretched across the table like something out of a dream. Roasted meats glistening with juices, platters of vegetables seasoned with herbs. Grapes, figs, and pomegranates spilled from silver bowls, and baskets of bread, still warm and fragrant, lay nestled between soft cheeses. The dark wine in crystal decanters shimmered, its scent heady and rich. Hunger clawed at me.

Lana hovered beside me, her gaze locked on the spread. "If this is a trap, it's the prettiest one I've ever seen," she murmured, her still trembling fingers brushing the edge of the

107

table. "Do you think it's safe?" Lana asked, her voice low and uncertain.

I shrugged, the gnawing ache in my belly clouding my judgment. "There's only one way to find out." I reached for a slice of meat. The moment it hit my tongue, the flavor burst like fire, smokey and rich, perfectly salted. A groan slipped from my throat before I could stop it. It wasn't just food—it was otherworldly.

Lana arched a brow, watching me carefully. "Well?"

I tore off another piece, chewing slowly to savor it. As if that was answer enough.

She hesitated for a second longer, then grabbed a hunk of bread and bit into it. The sigh she let out was almost indecent. "If this kills us, at least we'll die happy."

I laughed—a rare sound that surprised even me—and reached for more. A slice of pear, slick with honey, followed by a handful of grapes so ripe they burst in my mouth. Every bite was indulgent, every flavor sharper than anything I'd experienced before.

We found the wine next. Lana poured it into crystal goblets with a grin, handing me one without a second thought. "To . . . whatever this is." She lifted her glass.

I clinked mine against hers. "To making questionable decisions."

The wine was velvety on my tongue, leaving a slow burn in its wake. I drained half the glass in one go, the warmth spreading through my limbs, loosening muscles that had been wound tight for too long. Lana poured me another without asking, and we sat down on chairs that hadn't been there a moment ago but appeared as naturally as if they'd always belonged.

The food replenished. Bread slathered with soft cheese, roasted vegetables drizzled with oil, wine refilling faster than we could drink it. Each bite left me craving more, and we indulged like we hadn't eaten in days.

"So." Lana sighed between bites, her eyes twinkling with something playful. "Tell me about you. I mean, the real you. Not the wild, grumpy lone wolf that plays with traps."

Grumpy? I leaned back in my chair, rolling the wine on my tongue. "What do you want to know?"

She drew a breath. "How did you end up there? In the woods alone?"

I shrugged, setting my goblet down. "It's a long story."

"We've got time." She leaned forward, resting her chin on her hand. Her eyes gleamed with curiosity, and for the first time, I didn't mind the attention.

"I was born into Stikine Pack."

She frowned. "I've never heard of it."

I scoffed. "Count yourself lucky."

"Not a good experience?"

I shook my head. "My alpha was a brutal bastard. He was obsessed with control. Every breath we took had to be by his rules." The words flowed out of me with no resistance. It felt strange to say so much so easily.

"So you left."

That was a simplified version of events, but even though expressing myself felt easy in that moment, I didn't relish telling that story. How I'd battled my way out. How my mother had refused to come with me. Kael's and my story weren't all that different.

"I'm sorry." Her tongue flicked over her lips, and heat flashed under my ribs. My pulse kicked up, and my wolf stirred, prowling just beneath the surface. I cleared my throat, trying to ignore the way my skin prickled. Every movement Lana made pulled at me, tugging at something primal.

"What about you?" I asked, hoping the words would ground me.

She considered the question, her head tilting slightly, exposing the curve of her neck. My gaze locked on the delicate line, and my wolf growled low in my mind. *What the hell was happening to me?*

"Up until a year ago, I would've said my life wasn't dramatic," she answered.

"It is now?"

Lana shrugged, and reached for a piece of smoked meat. Her arm brushed mine, setting my nerves on fire. My fingers twitched, and I clenched my hands into fists, willing myself to stay still.

She placed the meat in her mouth. "I'm sure you've heard about what happened in Kitimat."

I forced myself to focus on her words, not the way her scent was wrapping around me. Earthy and warm. It was becoming impossible to ignore. I cleared my throat. "Rumors have made it up our way."

She patted the dagger on her hip, and my gaze dropped to the curve of her waist, lingering longer than I meant to. My wolf rumbled, pushing against my control, and I shifted in my seat to put some distance between us.

"They're now combined with what used to be my pack, Black Lake," she said.

I'd heard about Kitimat's alpha. I'd even found him up in our territory once. "And after seeing him exploit his pack, you still believe pack life is the answer?" The words slipped out, and even I was surprised I asked the question. Of course she did. She was still tied to her pack. She was here, searching for the relics of a new one.

Lana took another swig of wine, the movement drawing my attention to her lips. My eyes followed the path of a drop of red as it clung to the corner of her mouth. My wolf growled again, louder this time, and I shifted uncomfortably, feeling the heat spreading through my chest. Lower . . .

"We believe the same, I think," she said softly. I frowned, focusing on her words, but it was nearly impossible. "You want to help shifters," she continued. "What you do in the mountains is admirable, Destin, but you're only one wolf. You can't help everyone. A good pack can do that, and our job isn't only to protect our own."

I tore a piece of bread from the loaf on the table, needing something to do with my hands. Her words hung in the air between us. I shoved the bread into my mouth, chewing slowly, trying to block out the way her presence was seeping into me, making it impossible to focus.

"Humans," I muttered, forcing the word out through clenched teeth. "Right. Because they've been so understanding of our kind in the past."

I grabbed a slice of cheese, tearing into it with more aggression than necessary. My jaw worked, the sharp flavor doing little to distract me from the ache building beneath my skin. I needed to get a grip. "You live near them?" I asked. Up north, the only time I ran into humans was on purpose—which was never.

"I'm a teacher. I see them every day." She smiled. "I wanted to make a difference."

A wave of grief and guilt hit me, sharp and unexpected. It wasn't mine. I blinked, trying to push it back, but it clung to me, heavy and suffocating. "Doesn't seem like it's making you happy," I said, more bluntly than I intended.

Her eyes snapped to mine. "Why would you say that?"

I swallowed, suddenly too warm despite the cool air. I picked up my goblet, swirling the wine inside, watching the dark liquid spin. The truth slipped out before I could stop it. "I can feel what you feel."

Her eyes narrowed. "What do you mean?"

I exhaled slowly, rubbing the back of my neck. My wolf grumbled, restless under my skin, urging me to retreat, but there was no way to backtrack now. "I can sense emotions—anger, fear, joy. It's not something I can control."

Her gaze sharpened, and the intensity of her focus sent a shiver down my spine. "You're psi?"

I nodded, ignoring the strange swirling in my gut. Admitting it out loud made it feel too real, too exposed. *Why was I telling her this?* It wasn't unheard of for wolves to have special abilities, but this one . . . I'd been taught too many times to count that it wasn't appreciated.

"What do you feel from me?" she asked, leaning in slightly.

I hesitated, every instinct telling me to shut this down. Shifters didn't like their emotions laid bare, and I knew better than to dig where I wasn't invited. But Lana's expression was open, curious, and I couldn't seem to resist. "You want to know?"

She didn't answer, just waited, her eyes locked on mine. My wolf rumbled, more alert than ever, and I fought the urge to lean closer, to close the space between us. I chose my words carefully. I kept my observations strictly linked to the last two minutes of conversation.

"You're sad when you think about teaching," I said. "And you feel guilt."

Her lips parted slightly, and the sight of it made my pulse jump. "The school year is starting," she whispered. "I'm not there."

My wolf growled again, louder this time, and I felt the sharp edge of desire coil in my gut. Every movement she made —every tilt of her head, every flick of her tongue—was driving me closer to breaking. I adjusted in my seat, trying to find some relief, but there was no escaping it. She was in my head, under my skin, and the slow burn of the wine wasn't—

I blinked and glanced down. *The wine. The food.*

Lana leaned closer, her scent wrapping around me, and my breath hitched. "What else do you feel?"

I dragged a hand through my hair, my skin buzzing with tension. "Lana, I think—"

"Tell me," she whispered, and the softness in her voice sent a shiver down my spine.

I fought for breath. "I think the food is . . . affecting me." I swore under my breath, pushing my chair back and standing.

Lana blinked, her brows knitting together. "Affecting you how?"

I could've turned and shown her, but I didn't. If I saw her face, the last thread of my control was going to snap. The words felt thick in my mouth, my heart pounding harder. "I need to get some air. I need space. If I don't—"

I cut myself off, shaking my head as I stalked away from the table toward the trees.

But then Lana's hand wrapped around my arm, and she gave a gentle tug. I stopped dead in my tracks. "If you don't what?"

My whole body shuddered. "If I don't touch you, I'm going to—" I didn't know what I was going to do. Search for something to destroy? Spontaneously combust?

She rounded me, her expression unreadable as she stopped and tilted her chin to meet my eyes. Her pupils were dilated. Her cheeks flushed.

Thank the gods.

It wasn't only me.

CHAPTER
FIFTEEN

A slow, burning ache bloomed within me as I gazed at Destin. The wine still lingered on my tongue, sweet and heady. His eyes glinted with an intensity I'd never seen before. He was right. Our easy conversation. The heat building in my veins. It wasn't normal.

But even though I understood I was being acted upon, I didn't especially care. I lifted my hands and slid them over his chest. That movement alone sent ripples of pleasure over my skin, and I bit back a sigh.

We shouldn't do this. Destin and I weren't anything. We couldn't be anything. He was against the very mission I'd recently dedicated my life to. *Not dramatic.* It was almost laughable what my life had become.

But again. Right then? *I didn't especially care.*

What was it about this situation that made me want to throw caution to the wind? The wine? The food? The fact that we were in the middle of a mystical forest, and my wolf was suddenly rabid for his?

Not suddenly. She'd been paying attention to him since the first moment we saw him.

And you wouldn't listen, she snapped.

I almost laughed out loud. What was it about him—about his wolf—that was driving her mad? He was strong. Wild. The thought of him swinging his ax made me shiver.

I swallowed hard, my throat suddenly dry. "This is—"

Destin's lips twitched. "Mmhmm."

"Even after shots of whiskey, I've never . . . felt this." *Why was I still talking?* A slow breath slipped through my lips, and I realized my eyes were closed, my chin tilting so high, my back arched.

He reached out, his fingers brushing a strand of hair from my face, and my skin lit up like he'd struck a match. "Lana," he murmured, his voice a low rumble, and my wolf begged for him. My body begged for him.

My eyelids fluttered open. "This is probably a mistake."

"Probably." Destin's eyes darkened, and his hand slid to the back of my neck, pulling me closer. My breath hitched as our bodies pressed together, the hard planes of his chest against mine. His lips hovered over mine, and the heat of his breath on my skin made me melt like butter on a hot pan.

Time seemed to slow as he closed the distance, his lips brushing against mine. It was a feather-light touch, but it sent a shockwave of sensation through me. I gasped, and he took that for what it was. An invitation. His mouth crashed down on mine with a ferocity that stole my breath.

The already misty world around us disappeared as I melted into him. His hands roamed my back, pulling me closer, and I wrapped my arms around his neck, tangling my fingers in his hair. *Damn it, his unruly hair was so hot.*

His lips were rough and demanding, and I met him with equal intensity, pouring all my longing and frustration into that kiss. I clung to him, digging my nails into his shirt, wishing I could—

Dustin pulled back, his breath ragged. He glanced around, searching for something. My thoughts exactly.

The idea of sleeping in the woods should've given me a thrill, but I didn't want Destin on the pine needle-covered ground. Even if we couldn't feel it. The night air was warm, and my senses were lit up like a damn festival, and the only thing I wanted to do was lie down. *With him.*

Then it appeared. Out of nowhere, like a gift from the universe, a bed materialized. Not just any bed, but a masterpiece of nature. The frame was woven from thick, gnarled vines, interspersed with soft moss and trailing ivy. It looked like it had grown out of the ground, a living sculpture that had been there for centuries. The mattress was plump and inviting, covered in a quilt that seemed to be made from petals and leaves, stitched together with threads of gold.

Above it, a canopy of branches arched gracefully, their leaves forming a delicate lattice that filtered the moonlight into a soft, dappled glow. And then there were the lights. Tiny, ethereal orbs floated around the bed, twinkling like fireflies.

I took Destin's hand and stepped closer. It was like something out of a dream.

He pulled, turning me back toward him, and then his hands were at the hem of my shirt. The air was thick, almost syrupy. "Well, I guess that's one problem solved."

My heart beat against my ribs. "Only one?"

He dropped his head, pressing into my neck. "I still have to solve this one." He pulled my shirt up, dragging his hands over my bare skin, and I had to bite my lip to keep from gasping.

That's when I started to panic. "Destin, I—" My words

caught in my throat as his hand slid up my spine, his fingers underneath my bra clasp.

"You what?" He sucked my skin into his mouth.

I exhaled hard, my breath coming in short gasps as I tried to focus. "I don't think—taking a mate, that wouldn't—"

Destin pulled back. His eyes darkened, his pupils expanding until the green was almost completely eclipsed. He cupped my face with his hands, his thumbs brushing over my cheekbones. "I'm not looking to be owned by anyone."

Owned. The thought of being owned by him sent a spike of desire straight to my core. "Then what are we doing?"

Destin leaned in, his lips brushing against my ear. "We can do this without taking the bond. I won't mark you."

I shivered, my body responding to his words even as my mind tried to make sense of them. "How?"

He pulled back, his eyes dark and pupils blown wide. "Trust me."

The wolf in him took over, his movements insistent and feral. He gripped my shirt and pulled it over my head, then tore at his own clothing. *Wild.* His hands were on me again, his touch like fire against my skin. He found the clasp of my bra and unhooked it with a flick of his fingers, then slid it off my shoulders. I gasped as the warm evening air hit my bare skin, and he groaned, his hands sliding up my stomach to cup me.

I reached for him, fumbling with the button of his jeans. I couldn't think straight, couldn't focus on anything other than the need pulsing through my veins. I finally managed to get his pants undone, and he kicked them off, then pulled me against him.

The press of his bare skin against mine was electric, and I arched into him, my hands exploring the hair on his chest, his stomach, the tight V of muscle—

His fingers hooked in my waistband and yanked my pants

down, and I stepped out of them, my breath coming in ragged gasps. I was stripped mostly bare, standing in front of him, and I felt like the damn Venus with the way he looked at me.

Destin's eyes roved for one second longer, and his hands followed, exploring every dip and curve. He trailed his fingers over my hips, down my thighs, then back up to my waist. His thumbs hooked in the waistband of my underwear, and he paused, his eyes meeting mine.

I nodded, and he slid them down, exposing me completely. Destin's breath quickened, and he pushed me back, guiding me to the bed. The moment my legs hit the edge, I sank down onto the mattress, and he followed, his body covering mine. I slid my hand down, reaching for him, but he grabbed my wrists and pinned them above my head.

"Not yet," he growled, his voice rough with desire.

I whimpered, and he smiled, then lowered his head to my chest. I cried out as his mouth found my skin, his tongue swirling and flicking. My body arched off the bed. I was a whimpering mess by the time he kissed his way down my stomach, his hands gripping my hips. I couldn't think straight. I'd forgotten all about the mating bond or my responsibilities with the Shadow Pack or anything other than the fact that I needed him. *Now.*

Destin paused, his breath hot against my skin. I looked down at him, and his eyes met mine with a silent question. I nodded, unable to form words, and he didn't need anymore encouragement.

Destin's mouth descended, and I forgot how to breathe. It was like the universe had hit pause. Every breath, every touch, every heartbeat between us was amplified, echoing in the stillness of the forest. My mind was a whirlwind of awe, fear, and an overwhelming need that consumed every rational thought.

I thought I might come apart at the seams. My breath

hitched, and I bit my lip, trying to hold back the sounds that threatened to spill from my throat.

"Let go," he whispered, his voice rough. "I want to hear you."

I couldn't have held back if I'd tried. He lowered again, and I shattered, my body arching off the bed as waves of pleasure crashed over me. My wolf howled, and I reached for him, needing his weight. My hands gripped his shoulders, dragging him over me.

He was flushed, his breathing ragged. I loved that I could affect him as much as he affected me. I wrapped my legs around him, pulling him closer. He was everywhere, his scent, his touch, his breath on my skin. It was intoxicating. I was drunk on him.

Destin's lips were on mine, swallowing my cries, and I clung to him like a lifeline as our bodies finally connected.

"Okay?" he asked, his voice strained. I nodded, gasping.

He moved. Slow at first, and I matched his rhythm. And then it was *everything*. All at once. Gentle, raw, primal. He took his time, and I clutched at him, my fingers digging into his back, my thighs trembling. I was flying, tumbling, soaring above the trees, and when I finally plummeted back to earth, Destin was there shuddering with me.

He collapsed over me and we lay there, our legs tangled together, panting. The forest was quiet, the only sound the occasional rustle of leaves or the distant call of an owl. It felt like we were the only two people in the world.

"Yes." The word slipped out of me on a breath, and Destin tugged his fingers through my hair. Kissed my cheekbone with lazy, swollen lips.

"Yes."

CHAPTER
SIXTEEN

I shot up as if waking from a fever dream. My head throbbed dully, probably from the wine. I winced slightly and rubbed my temples. My memories were startlingly clear, not a blur like I'd feared.

I remembered everything. The taste of her. The feel of her skin against mine. The desperation and need. I turned to look at Lana, and she was already staring at me. Her cheeks were flushed as she clutched the sheets to her chest. Her hair fanned out around her, a dark halo against the pillow.

I took a breath, trying to steady myself. I wanted to say something, but the effects of the food and wine had worn off. The words didn't come easily anymore.

And my longing wasn't gone. Instead, there was a hollow ache in my center. We'd had a night together—an incredible night. That should have been enough to get her out of my

120

system. But I didn't feel satisfied, not in the least. I felt . . . disappointed.

My wolf lay with his head on his paws. Judging me.

I lifted my hand to reach for Lana, but before I could make contact, the world shifted beneath us.

The bed vanished. The forest along with it. All of it was replaced by the cold, hard ground of a cavernous chamber. The walls stretched up into darkness, and the air held a chill that seeped into my bones. I blinked, trying to make sense of the abrupt transition from intimate warmth to this vast, foreboding space.

Lana's breath hitched beside me, and I turned to see her standing where the bed had been, her hair no longer a tangled mess, her skin back to its usual hue. We were dressed. Clean as if we'd both washed in the creek. She looked as disoriented as I felt, her eyes wide as she took in the scene around her.

Your second challenge awaits. The voice echoed through the chamber, smooth and haunting. So that was it, then. Last night had been what? A reward? A trick? Probably that. We'd barely slept, and now Lana was being thrown back into the arena.

I turned to look behind me, and my breath caught. There, stretching out like a gaping wound in the earth, was a bottomless pit. It seemed to swallow the light, its edges jagged and unforgiving. Above it, suspended like a series of precarious stepping stones, were slabs of rock. Each one was etched with symbols, their surfaces worn smooth by time.

Lana took a step forward, her eyes narrowing as she studied the stones. "What is this?" she asked, her voice steady despite the tremor in her hands.

The light was still there, gently pulsing. *This is your test of knowledge and instinct. To cross the chamber, you must step on the correct stones in sequence. Each stone bears a mark from the lore of the Shadow Pack. Choose wisely, and you will proceed. Choose poorly, and you will face the consequences.*

I glanced at Lana, my pulse quickening.

She cleared her throat, her hands clenched at her sides. "What kind of consequences?"

The stones will only stay solid for a few moments. You must move quickly.

Lana's jaw tightened. The light faded as it had the day before, and her eyes flicked to mine. "Good morning."

Fear and uncertainty rippled through me. Her emotions. I grunted, my shoulders tense. I wanted to protect her from this. At least have a conversation about last night. But there wasn't time for that.

Lana took a deep breath and stepped onto the first stone. It flickered beneath her feet, the symbol etched into its surface glowing with a soft, otherworldly light.

Then, the riddle appeared, inscribed in the air above her in shimmering script.

IN THE DARKNESS, we thrive. In the light, we wither. What are we?

LANA FROWNED, her eyes darting to the stones ahead. She muttered something under her breath, and I strained to hear her. "Shadows. It's got to be shadows." She glanced back at me, and I gave her a nod. Was that too simple? What did that have to do with Shadow Pack lore?

Lana took a breath as the stone to her left lit up with her answer. She stepped forward, and the moment her foot made contact, the symbol on the first stone crumbled and dropped. The second stone held. She'd chosen correctly.

I exhaled, not realizing I'd been holding my breath. Another question blazed in the air.

I AM the howl that first broke silence, the moon that gave birth to night's kin. Without me, the wolves scatter; together, I bind what cannot be tamed. Who am I?

MY WOLF GROWLED, pacing in my head. He was worried for her. He'd been in my head all night, pressing forward toward her wolf, urging me to mark her. I'd fought him tooth and nail and actually won for once.

But now he was pissed. He wanted her safe. He wanted her *ours.*

"Alpha," Lana called out, and her eyes briefly flicked to mine. I clenched my jaw. So we were going to get some indoctrination along with this challenge. Fantastic.

Lana pressed on, her movements becoming more confident, but I could feel her uncertainty. Her wolf pushed her to act, to leap from stone to stone without hesitation, but she needed to think through each answer, and the questions weren't getting any easier.

With a glance back at me after the fifth question, she took another step. The stones were more unstable now. She hovered over the middle of nothing, the only stones behind her the wrong path. The stones ahead . . .

I dragged my hands through my hair, pacing as I watched. The air grew thicker, the silence oppressive. Lana's hair clung to her skin with sweat, and I could see the tremor in her muscles. She was on edge, her wolf instincts screaming at her to move faster, to leap and run, but she fought for calm. For control.

. . .

I LIVE *where the past lingers, woven through stories told in whispers and scars. I am a weight you must carry, yet release, to run free under the moon. What am I?*

LANA PAUSED, her chest heaving. She was panicking. She didn't know the answer. Her frustration and anxiety pulsed through me, and I clenched my fists, fighting the urge to do something. Anything.

"Breathe!" I called out. I was impotent there on the sideline and it was ripping me apart. The idea of her dropping into nothingness had my wolf pawing at the ground, baring his teeth.

I needed to calm down. To think. *I live where the past lingers, woven through stories told in whispers and scars.* It could be anything.

"Destin!" Lana's voice shook. She'd been standing there too long. The stone beneath her feet was beginning to waver.

What the hell was this challenge? How did solving riddles prove anything about Lana and Shadow Pack? The voice had said she'd be tested, but how many times? How long would we be stuck here? How many times would I have to stand here and watch?

I closed my eyes, forcing myself to let go. Fighting emotions never worked. I'd learned that younger than most since they'd threatened to consume me daily since I was a pup. I allowed my fear and Lana's to rush over me, sweeping through like a flooded river. I acknowledged the pain, the anxiety, the—

"Guilt!" I yelled, and Lana's eyes widened. Guilt. *You must carry, yet release to run free.* It worked. It had to work.

Lana spoke the word and stepped up to the glowing stone. It held. I dropped into a crouch, pressing my hands over my eyes, breathing with relief.

And then my eyes snapped open. Lana's emotions had passed through me, and mine were draining like water from a sink.

But there was another current. Another flow of . . . something. It was a slow hum, a pushing and pulling. I stood and turned in a circle, searching the cavern around us. There was nobody there, and yet—

My gaze caught on the stone beneath Lana's feet. I blinked. It was glowing, but that didn't mean it was sentient. Or could it be?

I closed my eyes, willing my body to still and feel. *Yes.* There was something there.

IN THE FOREST DEEP, a choice must be made,
One wolf stands alone, in shadow, afraid.
The pack howls a call, their strength in the night,
But the lone wolf's cry tugs at your heart's light.
If you run to the one, the many will fall,
If you stand with the pack, you answer the call.
What will you choose when the paths split in two?
The love of the one, or the pack that is true?

"WHAT KIND OF QUESTION IS THAT?" Lana growled, and her fear spiked. I was already moving. The voice in the light hadn't said a damn thing about me doing the challenge with her.

I skidded to a stop in front of the stones. Or the lack thereof. The only ones that were left were the wrong ones. I had no idea what would happen if I tried to step on them, which meant I had to find another way.

I scanned the side of the cavern wall, tracing the jagged edges with my eyes, calculating. There were outcroppings—barely—but enough to get a handhold if I was careful. Or stupid.

I charged forward and crouched down, running my hand over the rock face. There wasn't time to second guess it.

"Destin, what are you—"

Without giving myself more time to think, I swung one leg over the side of the stone and reached for a handhold on the cliff wall. My fingers scraped against the rough surface, finding just enough purchase. The moment my weight shifted from solid ground to the vertical rock face, my wolf snarled—half excited, half warning.

We fall, we die. No do-overs.

I gritted my teeth, pulling myself against the wall.

"What the hell, Destin!" Anger flared in Lana, and it was a welcome break from the fear. Good. Be pissed. It only added fuel to the adrenaline coursing through me.

Every inch was a fight. My fingers scraped against the stone, rubbed raw as I clung to the cracks and ridges. My boots scrabbled, and I shoved my toes into any crevice I could find.

One misstep and I'd be nothing but a wolf-shaped smear at the bottom of the abyss. I found a decent handhold just above me. The stone cut into my palm, but pain was better than falling. One hand over the other. One step at a time. The sound of my breath echoed back to me, loud and ragged in the cavern. I had no idea how much time had passed by the time I nearly pulled level with her. It couldn't have been long because the stone under her feet was still solid.

"You're going to get yourself killed!" she called out, her eyes wide.

"And you're not?" I hissed back. I glanced up. The wall stretched on endlessly above, but I wasn't aiming for the top. Just far enough to launch myself onto the stone where Lana stood. Easy. Totally doable.

I edged along the narrow ledge, muscles tight, breath measured. My heart pounded a wild rhythm in my chest—part adrenaline, part the wolf's maddening excitement. He always loved a gamble, especially the kind where death was on the table.

A rock slipped loose under my weight and tumbled into the abyss. My stomach flipped, and I dug in harder. I stole a glance toward Lana. She was still perched on that single stone—too far for a human to reach. But I wasn't just human.

My breathing quickened as I tensed. *You ready for this?* I asked my wolf. He gave me nothing but a hungry growl in response. Good enough.

My muscles tensed and my lungs locked in my chest. It had to be precise—no room for error. My wolf surged under my skin, eager to take control. He liked this. The thrill, the danger, the sheer insanity of it.

Just like I had in that cell, I let him take over. Without another thought, I kicked off the wall, every muscle in my body snapping into action. I launched myself through the air, the wind rushing past my ears, my heart hammering wildly in my chest. The stone loomed closer—too far, too close, all at once.

Lana gasped. My hands hit the edge of the stone, fingers digging deep into the jagged surface. My feet swung wildly over the void below, and for a split second, I hung there, suspended above nothing.

She swore under her breath as she crouched to steady herself against my landing. With a low growl, I hauled myself up.

Lana stumbled back as I landed beside her, panting, heart racing like I'd just outrun the apocalypse.

"Made it." I grinned as I tried to catch my breath.

"Made what, exactly?" she snapped, but there was relief in her voice, too. "Now there's two of us to fall?"

I closed my eyes, feeling for that current. Thankfully, since I'd already located it once, it was easier to find under the tumult. *There.* To our left. "Move. Now."

A retort started on Lana's lips, but I pulled her forward, and it fizzled. The stone lit up under our feet, and I coughed with relief. No more damn riddles and questions. We were doing this my way.

SEVENTEEN

Destin was in front of me, his movements sure and deliberate. *How was he doing this?* Every time a stone crumbled behind us, my heart skipped a beat, the abyss waiting below like it wanted to swallow us whole.

He glanced back, his eyes locking with mine for a brief moment. "This place—it works on energy."

I gripped his hand. "That means nothing to me!"

Somehow as we dashed over nothingness, he chuckled. "It means stop fighting it. Let it pull you."

"I'll let you pull me. How about that." I tried to match his movements, but every step felt like it would be the one that broke me. I was supposed to answer the riddles, not let Destin—not of the Shadow Pack—solve this for me. I had failed. I hadn't known the answers to the last two riddles. Destin had helped with the first, and now here I was, clinging to him and bypassing the rest.

If I didn't do this on my own, would it even count? The idea that we might get through this only for the test to reject us clawed at me. What if this was all for nothing? What if I was just dragging us both into—what? Back to the real world? Without the book?

Panic gripped me. I tried to shove the thoughts down, but they clung to me like the smell of bad fish.

A boom echoed through the canyon, and the rock walls shook. Destin's hand dropped mine to reach up and grip my arm like a vice. "Move!"

We leaped together, my feet barely finding purchase on the next stone before the last vanished into the void. I pushed myself forward, matching Destin step for step. Faster. We had to go faster.

I tugged on his arm, and we jumped to the next stone in sync, landing hard. Pain jolted through me, but I swallowed the lump in my throat and forced my legs to move. The stones blurred beneath us until finally, the end was in sight. A platform larger than the rest, shimmering with that same ancient energy. Relief surged through me.

We leaped together, landing on solid ground at last. The platform pulsed beneath our feet, steady and alive. I collapsed to my knees, my breath ragged, but Destin stayed standing, his gaze sweeping the space around us.

Tears pricked my eyes, and I dropped my head, trying to hide it.

Destin dropped to his knees. "Are you hurt?"

Our conversation from the night before landed heavily in my mind. Destin could feel this. He could sense all of it. That realization made the tears come faster, and I hated myself for it. "I'm fine."

"Obviously."

"Shut the hell up, Destin."

He cupped my jaw and tipped my face to his. "No. What's wrong?"

"I—" It took me a moment to collect myself. "I didn't do it. I didn't complete the challenge."

He frowned. "We're standing here. Safe." He motioned behind us, and I turned. The cavern was gone, replaced again by the smooth, calm forest.

"I realize that. But I didn't answer the questions. This was supposed to be a test."

Destin opened his mouth but didn't get a chance to answer. A wolf emerged from the shadows, its fur rippling like liquid night. It was huge, silent, its glowing eyes fixed on us with an unsettling calm.

Destin stepped in front of me without hesitation, his body tensing like a spring ready to snap. The wolf didn't growl, didn't make a single aggressive move. It simply stood watching us. Was this part of the test?

The wolf's eyes seared into me, and then it turned, padding away from us, its movements impossibly smooth. It didn't look back, but I knew. It wanted us to follow.

Destin hesitated for a moment before falling into step, and I followed close behind, my pulse racing. The landscape shifted as we moved, the oppressive darkness unraveling around us.

What had been dense forest opened into something far greater. Mountains stretched into the distance, their peaks gleaming like silver under a sky that shimmered with stars. Rivers wove through the landscape, carving out paths that seemed to lead to nowhere and everywhere at once.

It was breathtaking. Impossible. And I couldn't shake the feeling that we had stepped into something ancient, something sacred.

The wolf led us to the edge of a cliff, pausing as if waiting for us to understand something. Destin stood next to me, silent but not still. Every part of him was poised, aware. It hit me then. What I'd noticed the night before as I'd lain with my arms threaded under his.

He belonged here. In the real world, our world, Destin stood out. He was strange. Wild. But here? He seemed to blend in.

Now that I had a moment to breathe, the events of the night before pushed passed the morning's chaos. I shouldn't have done it—shouldn't have given in to the pull of whatever was in that wine.

Because last night, while it had been full of pleasure, it all felt empty in the light of day. I wanted more. And more wasn't what Destin was interested in. My wolf whined, and I mentally stroked her head. *I know, girl.* Regret tasted bitter on my tongue.

Destin turned his head slightly, probably sensing something in my thoughts, and for a brief moment, our gazes locked. The connection between us flickered. This time not from the wine.

The wolf gave a low huff, drawing our attention back to it. Without another word, it leaped from the cliff, disappearing into the mist below.

Destin stilled, then blew out a slow breath. "Could you see that before?"

I tracked ahead of where he pointed. "Holy shit." In front of us, through the trees, was Destin's cabin.

CHAPTER

EIGHTEEN

Destin

My house. We were staring at it when it had taken us days to come this far into the mountains. I took a step forward, and the ground seemed to pulse beneath my feet. I stumbled, catching myself on a nearby tree. "What the hell?"

Lana gaped. "Did the ground just move?"

I shook my head, trying to clear the fog. "Felt like it." I took another step, and this time, it was like the world morphed to meet me. I jolted again, but that time I was ready for it.

Lana put out her arms to keep her balance, then stepped up next to me. "It's like we're on a moving sidewalk."

I frowned. "A what?"

"You know, those things in airports? You stand on them, and they move you along?"

I shook my head. "Never been in an airport."

Lana blinked. "Seriously? Never?"

I didn't answer. I didn't need to.

Lana cleared her throat. "Okay, well, it's like that. But without the actual moving part." She took another step, and this time she didn't stumble.

"Makes perfect sense."

Lana elbowed me in the ribs. We took a step together. The ground seemed to stretch beneath us, like it was eager to carry us forward. It was disorienting but also exhilarating. In seconds we stood in front of my cabin, staring at the stacked wood pile.

I opened my mouth to say something, but she beat me to it. "We can go anywhere like this." She snapped her fingers. "We have to find Rowan and the others." Before I could argue, she grabbed my hand and started running.

"I still can't shift," she muttered as the world spun around us.

I'd already tried when that wolf had appeared. My wolf was aching to stretch his legs. We'd only been trapped here for what, thirty-six hours? It already felt like an eternity. Especially after last night . . .

My head swam with images. Flashes of Lana's skin, the memory of her breath. I wanted to drag her to a stop and have a repeat, but Lana was singularly focused on her friends.

I understood. Since we couldn't reach our packs, she hadn't been able to communicate with them. But verbal communication was the last thing on my mind right then.

Lana slowed, and I took in our surroundings as they settled. Power lines. Houses. We were standing in the middle of a road.

"This is Black Lake," she said. "Cmon."

We took a step, and we were in the town square. "Do you think they'll be here?"

"I have no idea," she murmured. Lana clenched her jaw, and my ribs cinched. She put on such a strong face, but I knew what was happening under the surface. She was nervous. Scared. Unsteady. I was the only one who knew those particular secrets, and it blew oxygen over the coals that were still simmering.

I felt everyone's emotions. This was nothing new. So why did it seem to matter so much that I felt hers?

Lana stopped next to what looked like a mechanic shop. She hesitated, then took one more step. I followed, and we passed through the walls.

"That's Tori, Mara, and Jasper," Lana whispered, though I was sure she could've shouted and it wouldn't have made a difference. The three shifters were in a tense conversation, and nothing we did seemed to impact the real world.

"You're sure?" Tori asked, her tone sharp.

Mara nodded, arms crossed over her chest. "Word came down from Blue Mountain. Shrikes were spotted just north of the river."

Jasper muttered a curse under his breath. "How close?"

"Close enough," Mara said grimly. "They're moving faster than we expected."

Tori ran a hand through her dark hair, frustration etched across her face. "We need a team on this. Now."

"Already stretched thin." Jasper's jaw was tight. "Rowan's gone north with the others. If we pull more wolves, we leave ourselves wide open."

Lana went rigid next to me. There it was again. *Guilt.* I was right there with her. We'd killed the shrikes that attacked us at the hostel. If there were more . . .

Mara exhaled. "We don't have a choice. If the shrikes are hunting, they won't stop at the river."

Jasper blew out a breath, his voice dropping lower. "It'll

have to come from Chilliwack. They've got the numbers, barely."

Tori chewed her lower lip. "I agree. And if they hesitate?"

Jasper's eyes darkened. "Then I go myself. And you have to explain that to Blake."

Lana gripped my arm and pulled me out of the shop. "North. They're already gone."

We followed the road back the way we came, our steps eating up the distance in a matter of minutes. The buildings grew sparser, giving way to the natural landscape of northern British Columbia. I took a deep breath, the crisp air filling my lungs. I could almost taste the snow, and it was only September.

I felt a pull to the east. To my cabin, my territory. I needed to make sure those dark creatures weren't anywhere near the wolves there. But Lana was singularly focused, and I wasn't going to leave her side in this place.

A few moments later we were at a hotel. Lana hunted around, then nodded for us to continue. It didn't take long for me to realize where we were heading next, and soon we stood in front of it. The old building the alphas had used as their temporary headquarters. The place where they'd held me captive.

"They're here." Lana pointed at the door. It hadn't fully closed, not that we needed it to be unlocked. Again we stepped forward, passing through the walls like smoke.

"—don't see anything that would give that impression," Callista said, her voice tight with worry. "There's nothing up there." She had a tablet in her hand, and her fingers were flying over the screen.

"I don't give a damn if it's in the records," Rowan growled. "Kael, did he give you any idea where he was taking her?"

Us. They were talking about us.

Kael shook his head. "I'm sorry. We didn't know how long the scent would last."

Evelyn waved him off. "I'm glad you came when you did. It was hard enough to track you when it was fresh, and this . . ." She shook her head. "It's not the same. They're masking it differently."

Callista turned the tablet to face them. "This is her last known location. Her phone is dead, so I don't know . . . They might be somewhere else by now."

"Without her phone?" Evelyn looked skeptical. She blew out a breath, then motioned for the others to follow her. She walked straight toward us, and as I braced for her to pass through, she stopped. Her brow furrowed, and she lifted her nose into the air. Then she blinked and kept walking.

"Destin?" Lana kept her voice low. I turned to face her. "Let's go check on them."

"On who?"

"Your wolves."

My wolves. I bristled. "They're not—"

"Right. I know." Lana gave me a look, then waited for me to take the lead.

We left the building, and the forest blurred past us. I couldn't explain how I knew where to go, but I felt it. Could sense it.

In seconds, we reached the clearing where the first cabin sat, its rough-hewn logs blending seamlessly with the surrounding forest. I slowed, then took a step so I could look through the windows.

The family was inside. Smiling. No sign of a disruption. I exhaled, my shoulders relaxing slightly. We did a loop of the perimeter in three steps. "Next."

We followed the same pattern with three more cabins and two yurts. Fine. They were all fine. But then as we approached the next cabin, my wolf perked up. *I sense it, too, boy.* Something felt off.

I couldn't put my finger on it until finally, I noticed the bare tree branches. No birds. They were gone.

"Destin—"

I held up a hand, and Lana silenced. I couldn't hear anything. *Not a damn thing.* I took her hand and pulled her another step, just like we'd looped around the other houses. That's when I saw it. High on the incline.

Bone stalker.

Its gaunt, skeletal form slinked through the underbrush. Its bleached-white skin seemed to glow in the dim light, and *those eyes.*

There was movement inside the cabin. This one housed a lone she-wolf. I motioned for Lana to stay put, but she didn't listen. Of course she didn't listen. She stepped up next to me, her gaze hardening as she saw the creature. "How can we stop it?"

I shook my head. "I don't know." We hadn't been able to touch our packs. We could move through walls. If I charged, I'd go right through the damn thing.

The bone stalker moved with an unnatural grace, its limbs bending at odd angles as it targeted the cabin.

I clenched my fists, my anger boiling over. I had to do something. "Your friend. I think she sensed something back there. Maybe that thing will, too." I pulled her forward until we stood right in it's path, then moved to the side, hoping it would catch our scent and change direction.

It didn't. Didn't even pause. That's when I launched myself forward and ended up flat on the unnatural forest floor so far away from Lana, she looked like she could fit in my hand. The bone stalker hadn't even felt me.

I pounded my fists against the ground, my knuckles

screaming. Then I forced myself up. I couldn't do it. Couldn't save her.

I stepped forward to find Lana, but blinked. Where had she gone?

There. Directly in front of the bone stalker. She had the dagger in her hand, and as she slashed forward, the world ahead rippled. It was subtle, almost imperceptible, but I saw it. Like a shiver down someone's spine.

Lana's head shot up, searching for me. "Destin!"

I was already running, nearly slamming into her after two steps. "What did you do?"

Lana tried to catch her breath. "I don't know. I think the relic—maybe we can't pass through, but it can?"

I stared at the bone stalker still treading toward the cabin. "The dagger won't kill it."

Lana nodded. "I know. It slowed it down in the mountains, but it didn't stop. The best way to kill dark creatures is fire."

"But you don't have a fire relic."

Lana blinked. "I made the bed appear."

My brow pinched. "What?"

Her hands were moving in front of her, the dagger swinging. "I thought about it. I thought about how much I wanted —" She caught herself, swallowing hard. "I thought about it, and it was there. Maybe with the fire, it would be the same thing?"

Lana's cheeks flushed, but she closed her eyes, holding her arms out.

"Lana, what the hell are you doing?"

"I don't know!" she snapped. "Trying something."

I couldn't blame her for that, but the bone stalker was getting dangerously close to the cabin. "Lana—"

"You said this place works on energy, correct?"

"Yes."

"Then teach me."

"Teach you what?"

Her eyes flew open. "How to feel it. How to move with it. Whatever the hell you were doing with the stones!"

I gaped at her. I was supposed to teach her in thirty seconds something I'd never even fully understood myself? *I'm trying something.* If she was willing, I could be, too.

I huffed out a breath, then reached out and took her hands. "Close your eyes." She did as I asked. "Imagine the earth beneath you. Feel its pulse, its rhythm." Her eyelids flickered. "Breathe."

I waited, not sure if she was feeling anything other than her own blood pumping through her veins. I pretended she could. "Good. Now, instead of fighting it, let it flow through you. Like a conduit."

She frowned. "A conduit?"

"Like a riverbed. The water flows through, but the riverbed doesn't try to control it. It guides it."

She nodded. "Okay, so I'm the riverbed."

"Yes. Now, focus on what you want to create. Fire. Heat. Let that intention guide the energy." Saying the words out loud made me nervous. It was one thing to admit I had the capability, another to admit what ran through my head. It sounded too mystical. Too . . . hippy-dippy. Even for those of us who knew magic existed.

Nothing happened.

Lana cursed. "This isn't working, Destin. I can't—"

"Shh." I moved behind her, wrapping my hands over the front of her hips. "Don't force it. Let it flow." We didn't have much time. The stalker was at the house. It was sniffing its way to the front steps.

She gritted her teeth. "I feel it. But it's not flowing. It's just . . . stuck."

That's when I closed my eyes. I ran my hand under the hem of her shirt, flattening it over her stomach. "Remember last night?"

"Mmm." Her breathing quickened.

"You wanted to be in control, and then—" My eyes snapped open at a sudden whoosh. A tendril of flame licked up from the ground in front of us. It wasn't like any fire I'd ever seen. It was pure, white-hot, with hints of blue at the tips."Holy shit, Lana. That was fast."

"Yeah, well." Lana exhaled, sinking into me for one more moment, then threw herself forward, carrying the flame with her.

I didn't know how I conjured the fire, but I knew what it felt like. As soon as Destin had forced me out of my head, something hollowed out within me. Like I was an empty vessel. A conduit he'd called it.

Let me help, my wolf growled.

Gladly.

In seconds I was on the bone stalker, slashing first with my dagger, then hurling the flame forward. The creature felt something—it knew I was there and recoiled from the heat. I felt a rush of triumph.

More. I followed Destin's advice and opened myself up again, reaching with the dagger until there was an open, vibrant slash in the haze. I pushed the flames forward, and they surged, wrapping around the creature like serpents.

It screeched, its skeletal body writhing. The flames consumed it, and within moments, there was nothing but ash.

I released the energy, and the fire winked out, the sky slowly fading back to murk. My knees wobbled, and I swayed on my feet.

Destin's solid arms wrapped around me, and I leaned into him, my breath coming in ragged gasps. When my thoughts settled, I looked up at him, my heart finally beginning to slow. "Thank you."

My gratitude felt long overdue. I wasn't used to having help like this. Yes, I had my pack. I had Rowan and Jasper, Evelyn, Callista, and Kael. They all had my back, but this . . . This felt different.

He shook his head. "I didn't—"

"Destin, spare me the humility. You were a badass on the steps and then you taught me how to light that bastard up. Thank you."

The corner of Destin's mouth curled. He wet his lips. "You're welcome."

My heart was no longer settling. "I'm glad you stayed." Blood rushed from my limbs at the admission. It didn't have to mean anything. The words themselves weren't damning. But Destin could feel what was happening in my head and my heart.

I stepped back from him, dropping my eyes to the ground. "Is there anyone else we need to check on?"

Destin cleared his throat. "We don't know where the other bone stalkers are."

"I know. Do you think—" I didn't finish my sentence. Ahead of us bloomed the same ghostly light.

No. I wasn't ready for another challenge. My bones were heavy with exhaustion, my eyes already drooping. I wanted to speed through the trees and go back to our forest. Our quiet place with the trees, the rocks, and the fairytale bed.

But maybe that was the point.

Destin turned and followed my gaze. His nostrils flared.

"What will it be this time?" I murmured.

He drew a breath and exhaled, then reached out and took my hand. I gripped him tightly as we walked forward.

That time as we approached, there was no otherworldly voice. The light diffused like mist, and in the center was a single, glowing orb. My pulse quickened as we drew closer. Would we be thrown into another treacherous obstacle course? A battle arena? I shivered, thinking of the two bone stalkers we still didn't have a location on.

The orb hovered in front of us, and I stopped watching its slow, rhythmic pulse. Destin stood next to me, not speaking. I didn't have his psi abilities, but it was disturbing how well I was beginning to read him. His silences were nuanced. Specific. Comfortable.

I inspected the orb, waiting for it to do something, but it only hung in the air. My wolf prowled, watching, waiting. On high alert.

Then I felt a tug. A string pulling me toward it. I reached out with a trembling hand, my fingers brushing the air. I didn't know why I was doing it, didn't understand the compulsion, but I couldn't stop.

My heartbeat thundered in my ears as my fingertip neared the light. The air around it was warm, as if I were reaching toward a slow-burning fire. My wolf growled low in my chest, a mix of curiosity and caution.

I hesitated for a split second, then pushed forward, my finger pressing against the surface of the orb. It was like a bubble, and when my fingers finally broke through, it felt like dipping into a pool of liquid silk, smooth and enveloping.

Warmth flooded through my arm, and there was a flash, a plunge as if I'd dropped beneath the surface of a lake, and then the world snapped back into focus.

I gasped, my lungs sucking in a breath.

The light was gone, and I was back where we'd started. There were the trees. The place where the table had been. And—

My heart sank like a stone. "Destin?" I whirled, reaching out my hand as if touch could find him when my eyes couldn't. "Destin!" I called louder, but my voice echoed back to me without a reply.

He was gone. And I had no idea where to find him.

CHAPTER
TWENTY

DESTIN

My breath left my lungs in a rush, and I blinked, my eyes stinging as they adjusted to the light. I was lying on the ground next to the sacred stone. A shudder ran through me as I realized I was naked. The ground was cold against my skin, and the air bit at my exposed flesh.

I pushed myself up, my head swimming as I tried to make sense of what had just happened. The stone. The relic. *Where the hell was Lana?*

My heart raced, and I pushed up from the ground, searching the clearing for any sign of her. I stumbled forward, pressed my palm out toward a tree trunk, and hit solid wood. *No.* This wasn't the realm I'd been in. This was the real world.

All the sensations rushed in. Aches. Pains. Hunger. *When was the last time I'd eaten?* That feast had somehow sustained us for days, but now that I was back in my reality, pangs hit my stomach.

I charged back to the stone, my mind racing as I slapped my palm down. "Lana?" My voice echoed in the clearing, but there was no response. Panic clawed at my throat. She was alone. She'd touched the glowing light, and now she was alone there. I let out a guttural yell, my chest so tight, I thought my ribs might splinter.

It was then that I heard it. The soft crunch of leaves underfoot. I spun, my muscles tensing as I faced the source of the sound.

A figure emerged from the shadows, and my blood ran cold. It was a man, tall and broad-shouldered, with dark hair and piercing blue eyes. His chiseled features were set in a mask of indifference, but I knew better.

James. My old Alpha.

Every instinct in my body screamed at me to run, to get the hell out of there, but my legs were like lead. Memories slammed into me, one after the other, of the nights I'd spent under his control. The humiliation, the pain, the fear. His alpha energy rolled over me in waves, pushing me back into the meek boy I'd been then.

"Destin." His voice was a low growl, and I flinched.

I forced myself to meet his gaze, my hands clenched into fists at my sides. "What are you doing here?"

James' lips curled into a cruel smile. "I could ask you the same thing, but I already know. I see you've found yourself a nice little plaything."

Rage bubbled up inside me, but I swallowed it down. I couldn't let him see how much his words affected me. I couldn't show him anything. If there was one thing I'd learned under James' thumb, it was how to be a blank slate. How to be numb.

"I visit this site for fun." I spit the last word, hoping he'd read between the lines.

James chuckled, and the sound grated against my nerves. "Oh, that doesn't surprise me." He strode to a boulder at the edge of the small clearing between the rock faces and sat.

I stood there, naked, my mind spinning in a thousand directions. Why had I been pulled out of the realm? Why then? *And what was happening to Lana?*

I called for her again, hoping that even if I couldn't see or hear her, she could hear me. I waited for a ripple from her dagger. For a scent that I could discern like her friend had earlier. But there was nothing.

"I'm so glad you remembered this place. I hoped it had made an impression." James smiled up at me, and that image dropped me back into my life in his pack. I could still feel the sting of his hand against my cheek, the taste of blood in my mouth as he punished me for disobedience. His voice, dripping with disdain as he gave me orders I couldn't disobey.

I remembered the shame that washed over me as I watched him impose his will, making me follow orders like a trained dog. He'd forced me to submit, to bow to his authority, and I hated myself for it.

My stomach twisted at the memory. He'd forced me to attack my own pack mates. To sink my teeth into their flesh, to draw blood, to assert dominance that wasn't mine to claim. He'd reveled in watching me suffer. A sadistic pleasure, a hunger for control. He enjoyed breaking me, enjoyed watching me writhe under his thumb.

The night I left my pack had been just like this one. Cool. Autumn. My breath fogged in the night air, and the crunch of leaves under my paws felt like a drumbeat. I had to be silent. I had to be quick.

Every step I took away from my family felt like a betrayal.

I'd promised to protect them, to be there for them, but I couldn't do it under James. So I ran. I didn't stop until I was miles away, until the scent of my pack was a distant memory.

The forest became my home. I learned to track, to hunt, to survive on my own. I found solace in the isolation, in the silence of the trees. But I never forgot my family. I never forgot the faces of the wolves I'd left behind.

By the time I felt strong enough to go back, they'd forgotten me. Now, standing in that clearing, I felt that same sense of guilt. Of abandonment. I'd brought Lana here, and now I was powerless to protect her. To protect any of them.

And then, in an instant, those memories shattered as two figures emerged from the slot in the stone walls. The second Alpha was lean, wiry, with calculating eyes. The third was massive, towering over the others with a perpetual scowl etched into his features. But it wasn't their presence that made my blood run cold. It was who they dragged with them.

Kael. Callista. Rowan. Evelyn. The four of them were bound, their faces contorted in pain. My wolf growled low in his throat, his hackles raised as emotions washed over me. Their fear, their confusion, and most of all, their pain.

They couldn't shift. I could see it in their eyes, the desperation as they tried to call their wolves and found nothing. It was then that I noticed the threads around their wrists. Thin. Strong. I had no doubt it was laced with the same compound I used in my traps in the forest.

Since I'd learned about it from him in the first place.

"You sick son of a bitch," I growled, the words barely a whisper.

I wanted to tear all three of them apart. To rip their throats out and watch the life drain from their eyes. Just as I was about to lunge for the wiry alpha closest to me, two more figures emerged from the woods, their eyes glowing red.

The bone stalkers stopped on either side of Kael, and James stepped forward, his lips curling into a cruel smile. "This will all be very simple. You don't have to do a thing."

Tree branches rustled above me, and I looked up. Dark wings. Shrikes.

James leaned forward, his piercing eyes locked onto mine. "Well, I have to admit, it was almost too easy." His voice was smooth and cold.

I searched for my pack. I was starting to shiver, but I wasn't going to admit it.

James pushed up to stand, his eyes never leaving mine. "We knew Kael would come for you. It was only a matter of time." He paused, letting his words sink in. "So, we left out a few clues. We figured if he hadn't come back for the dagger, he knew what it was and probably had ideas about what else we were after."

"We weren't sure who would come here once they found the information on that slip of paper, but Kael knows your history. And you, being the dutiful protector that you are, would most likely lead whoever it was right in." He spread his arms wide, as if presenting the scene before us. "And here we are."

He sighed with satisfaction. "I am jealous, though. You succeeded where I could not." His eyes dropped to the stone. To the smooth, clean surface that didn't show any evidence of Lana's blood.

My wolf pushed forward, urging me to shift. To attack. But if I did, those bone stalkers would tear Kael apart before I could get to him. He had no defense.

James stopped a few feet in front of me, his voice dropping to a whisper. "Ironic, isn't it? That your desire to protect has brought you to this point of utter helplessness." His smile faded. "You have no idea how long I've been waiting for this.

How many sacrifices I've made. But now, it's finally within reach."

I took a step forward, my hands curling into fists. I didn't know what information he had. He hadn't seen Lana as far as I knew. How could he know where she was? I wasn't going to give him any more information that could be used against us.

I threw my arms out wide. "I don't know what you were hoping to get. But I don't have it."

James raised an eyebrow. "I can't lose, you know. If she succeeds, I'll be here to greet her when she steps out with the relic. If she fails, well . . ." He shrugged. "She has family, doesn't she? It shouldn't be too hard to find more with her bloodline."

CHAPTER

TWENTY-ONE

Lana

The light was back, and I didn't wait for it to speak. "Where is he? What did you do to him?" I was hyperventilating, imagining Destin back in his cell or with the bone stalkers.

My wolf clawed against my consciousness. *Find him.* Her voice rang in my head like a gong.

It is admirable that you worked together to face these tests. A Shadow Pack leader must be humble and inspire their pack. But this final challenge is yours alone.

My eyes widened, and my voice broke as I demanded, "Tell me he's safe."

Daughter, the wolf is back where he belongs, and you are home. A place he cannot be. The shadow realm is a sanctuary for protectors. It is where your bloodline can be most effective, where you can fulfill your purpose. Other wolves do not belong here.

152

I thought of the riddles, and the truth of the Shadow Pack began to coalesce. They lived here? Beyond the veil of our world? "Why did they leave?" I asked. How had they left? I'd streaked the dagger relentlessly and barely made a tear in the fabric of this realm.

You are home.

I turned in a circle, taking in the wood that had once felt comforting with Destin by my side. Now it only felt empty. Depressing.

"I don't want to be here alone—I'm not ready to be alone." My voice was barely a whisper, but there was nobody there to hear it.

The light and the voice had already vanished. My breaths came in shallow, rapid bursts, and my wolf's senses went into overdrive. She sniffed the air, her ears twitching at every creak and whisper of movement. She was desperate to find him. Desperate to protect him.

Mist again swirled around me, and a chill crawled up my spine. *Final challenge.* At least I knew it was ending. But how it would end . . .

The world shifted, and I barely flinched. Over the past two days, my body had adapted to the strangeness of this place.

Out of nowhere, mirrors appeared. They lined the walls, their silvery surfaces reflecting the mist and shadows. I turned in a slow circle, feeling a magnetic pull toward one of them. My feet moved on their own, carrying me closer until I stood directly in front of it.

The surface rippled like water, and I was enveloped in cool air. Like I was being sucked below the surface of a lake.

I stood in my childhood home. In the living room, to be exact. The familiar beige couch and dark wood coffee table sat in front of me, and the smell of my mother's lavender air freshener filled my nostrils. I heard footsteps, and my father's voice boomed from the hallway.

"Lana, what is this?" He held up a slip of paper, his face a mask of disappointment. I knew what it was before he even said it. My report card.

I swallowed hard. "I tried my best, Dad. It's just one grade—"

"One grade? One grade can be the difference between success and failure, Lana. You need to work harder." His eyes bore into mine, and I felt that familiar pit open up in my stomach.

"I'm sorry, I—"

"Your brother never has these issues. He brings home straight A's. Why can't you be more like him?"

I clenched my fists. I wanted to scream that I was trying, that I was doing everything I could to make him proud. But the words caught in my throat.

My father turned and walked away, leaving me standing there, my heart in pieces.

This wasn't real. I swallowed the lump in my throat, finding comfort in the details. The framed photos on the mantel, the patterned rug under my feet, the curtains my mother had sewn herself.

Then I slammed back into my body and staggered, struggling to catch my breath. The mist around me thickened, and I was dragged like iron filings to a magnet toward another mirror. I tried to resist, but it was like fighting a strong current.

My fingers brushed the glass, and the world shifted again. This time, I was standing in the middle of a crowded room. Music pounded through my skull, the bass reverberating in my chest. Strobe lights flickered, and I looked down to find a red Solo cup in my hand, the liquid inside sloshing as I moved. The scent of alcohol and sweat filled my nostrils, the buzz of the drink coursing through my veins. I was at a college party. One of many I'd attended during those years.

A laugh bubbled up from my throat, and I found myself grinning at a joke I couldn't remember hearing. My eyes were unfocused, my vision hazy from the combination of alcohol and the swirling lights. I turned and saw a guy standing next to me, his arm draped over my shoulders. His breath was hot against my ear as he whispered something I couldn't make out over the music.

My skin prickled as his hand slid down my arm, his fingers brushing against my hip. I didn't flinch. Didn't pull away. In that moment, I didn't care. I was numb. That was the whole point of going to those parties, wasn't it? To forget.

I wanted to forget everything. Who I was. What I was capable of. *The voice inside my head.*

My phone buzzed in my pocket, and I ignored it. It was probably my pack mates wondering where I was. Wondering why I wasn't at the latest training session or pack meeting. I told myself I didn't care. That I needed a break, that I was allowed to have fun.

The guy's hand slipped lower, resting on my thigh, and I still didn't move. My wolf stirred, but I pushed her down. I didn't want to think about what she wanted. What I should've been doing instead of getting drunk and letting some guy grope me in the middle of a crowded room.

My phone buzzed again. And again. I frowned and pulled it out, squinting at the screen. The words blurred together, and I had to blink several times before they came into focus.

LANA, it's your brother. He's in the hospital.

. . .

THE ROOM SPUN AROUND ME, the music fading to a dull throb in the background. I read the message again, my brain struggling to process the words. Hospital. Brother. The guy next to me said something, but his voice was muffled, like I was underwater.

I stumbled back, the cup slipping from my fingers and spilling its contents on the sticky floor. His hand fell away, and I pushed through the crowd, my heart pounding in my ears. I needed to get out. I needed to breathe.

I burst through the front door, the cool night air hitting my face like a slap. I leaned against the railing, my mind racing. My brother. In the hospital. I hadn't even known he was sick. How could I not know? What kind of sister was I?

I drew a shaky breath, my eyes stinging with tears. I'd been so wrapped up in my own world, in my own pain, that I'd neglected the people who mattered most.

The music faded as I dropped back into myself. I shook as I stared at my reflection. So tough, Lana. So strong. Nothing ever fazed her. She was the Black Lake third. She was—

I wanted to scream as a third mirror came into view. I was sucked into a dimly lit room, the curtains drawn to block out the harsh afternoon sun. I sat on the edge of the bed, my brother's hand limp in my grasp. The air was thick with the scent of antiseptic and something metallic and sterile that clung to the back of my throat.

His chest rose and fell with labored breaths, each one a battle against the muscles that refused to cooperate. His skin clung to his bones, stretched taut like a drum. I could see the outline of his ribs, the way his collarbone jutted out from his neck. His eyes, once so full of life, now stared up at the ceiling with a dull resignation.

I reached over and adjusted his pillow, trying to make him more comfortable. His head lolled to the side, and I winced at the sight of the tube inserted into his nostril. "Do you need water?" I asked, my voice barely above a whisper.

He shook his head, and I felt a pang of guilt for even asking. Of course, he didn't need water. He didn't need anything. His body was shutting down, piece by piece, and there was nothing I could do to stop it.

Shouldn't his magic save him? Heal him from this? A tear slipped down my cheek, and I quickly brushed it away. I didn't want him to see me cry. He'd seen enough pain already. "I'm sorry I wasn't here sooner." My voice trembled. "I should've been here. I should've known."

His fingers twitched in mine, and I looked up to see his eyes on me. "It's not your fault," he croaked, his voice barely audible.

I shook my head, unable to accept his forgiveness. "It is my fault. I was too wrapped up in my own shit."

He squeezed my hand with what little strength he had left. "Lana, it's not your fault."

I swallowed hard, my throat constricting. I wanted to tell him it wasn't fair. That he deserved better. But the words felt hollow. Empty.

He closed his eyes, a tear slipping down his cheek. "I don't want to die, Lana." The raw emotion in his voice shattered me.

I leaned in, pressing my forehead to his. "I know. I know." My voice cracked, and I felt his breath warm against my skin. "But you're not alone, okay? I'm here. Mom and Dad are here. We're all here."

He nodded, his breath ragged. "I'm scared."

I pulled back, my eyes locking onto his. "You're the bravest person I know. You always have been."

He tried to smile, but it came out as a grimace. "I don't feel brave."

"You don't have to feel it to be it." I squeezed his hand, my heart aching. "And when it's time, I'll be right here with you. I promise."

He nodded again, his eyes fluttering closed. I watched him, my chest tight with grief and love and a thousand other emotions I couldn't name. I wanted to take his pain away. To give him a future. But all I could do was sit there and hold his hand as he slipped away.

The memory faded like the others, and I was left standing in the mist, my heart in pieces. I wanted to scream at the injustice of it all, to demand answers from the universe. My wolf howled in my chest, her grief and rage mirroring my own. She wanted to hunt, to kill. But there was no enemy to fight, no prey to bring down.

The air grew colder, the mist thickening, and I hugged my arms around myself. The silence was deafening, pressing in on me from all sides. Then, like a whisper carried on the wind, I heard it.

Shadow Pack blood has always been hidden in weakness.

I spun around, searching for the light, but saw only the swirling haze. A broken sob ripped from my chest. "Show yourself!"

When I got no response, I fell to my knees, burying my face in my hands. I couldn't save him. Our magic couldn't save him.

What if I told you, Lana, that you could save him now?

The world seemed to grind to a halt. I sucked in a breath, my heart clenching. "He's gone."

The mist swirled around me, closing in. *Shadow Pack is never truly gone.*

For a moment, I couldn't breathe. My wolf's ears perked up, and she stopped pacing, her eyes fixed on a point in the distance. The voice was coming from everywhere and nowhere, wrapping around us like a shroud.

You could bring him back. Bring him to you.

My wolf whined, and I felt her longing, her desperation to reach out and grasp what the presence was offering. I wanted it. I wanted it so badly.

I rose to my feet, wiping my cheeks. *Yes.* I wanted to scream the word out loud, but before my mouth opened, I stilled.

This was a test.

Why show me the mirrors? Why force me to relive these memories? "You're lying."

Cool air swirled around me. *I am bound by truth.*

Shadow pack blood has always been hidden in weakness. The words repeated in my mind, and a chill ran down my spine. My brother had been weak. He'd been vulnerable. And now I could fix that?

The surface of the mirror shimmered, and there he was. Standing in front of me. My brother, strong, upright on his own two feet. I rushed forward and pressed my hand against the glass.

THE MATE OF THORNE MOREAU, *once stricken with disease, then revived with wine from the everlasting goblet.*

I BLINKED. Those were words from my storybook.

THE ALPHA AND THE CROWN. *No wolf's mind is his or her own.*

SOMETHING TICKLED the back of my mind. One wolf. No, lone wolf? Words sat on the edge of my tongue, then finally sprang into perfect, impossible clarity.

· · ·

IN THE FOREST DEEP, a choice must be made,
One wolf stands alone, in shadow, afraid.
The pack howls a call, their strength in the night,
But the lone wolf's cry tugs at your heart's light.
If you run to the one, the many will fall,
If you stand with the pack, you answer the call.
What will you choose when the paths split in two?
The love of the one, or the pack that is true?

THE ONE OR THE MANY. That was the test. But just like in the second challenge, I didn't know what answer I was supposed to choose.

Both options felt right—and wrong.

The weight of the decision pressed down on me. The lone wolf, isolated and afraid, called to something primal within me. *Alone.* How could I leave someone behind in the dark when I had the power to help them? If I chose the pack over the one, wouldn't I betray the very essence of what it meant to lead? Weren't we supposed to protect those who needed us most?

But then there was the pack. A wolf without a pack was as good as dead. Strength came in numbers, and the safety of the whole outweighed the safety of one. That was the harsh truth we were taught as pups: the pack must always come first, because when the pack fell, everyone did. If I gave in to my desire to save the lone wolf, the many would suffer—and how could I live with that?

I closed my eyes, breathing deeply. I imagined both outcomes playing out. Running toward the lone wolf meant leaving the pack vulnerable. But ignoring the lone wolf felt just as monstrous.

My wolf stirred uneasily inside me, conflicted.

It was my brother. Truth washed over me. I'd go to him every time. But that terrified me because it wasn't what a pack wolf would do. It was what a lone wolf—an outsider—would do.

I gritted my teeth, frustration twisting in my gut. This wasn't just about the riddle. It was about what kind of wolf I wanted to be. What kind of wolf I *was.*

THERE ONCE WAS *a man named Thorne Moreau . . .*

I STEPPED BACK from the mirror, my hand shaking. "No. This power, the relics, none can be used selfishly." If I used the goblet to save one wolf I loved, when would it stop? I would be just as bad as Thorne. Using the relics to play god, to get whatever I wanted.

That couldn't have been why they were created.

The mirror's surface swirled, and a fourth time, I was dragged forward. The mist around me thickened, and I was drawn in like a leaf caught in a whirlpool.

This time, when I emerged on the other side, the air was different. Thicker. Heavier.

And then I saw them. My friends. Evelyn, Kael, Callista, Rowan, and—

I gasped. *Destin. Bone stalkers.* They stood in the gap between the rock faces, the stone at Destin's back. He was nude. Shaking. Three men I didn't recognize faced him.

This wasn't real. The words felt hollow when I thought them. There were our backpacks. Evelyn was wearing the same shirt she'd had on in the building.

How much time had passed? We'd moved through this realm in short bursts, but what had happened beyond this veil?

Callista winced, and my eyes shot to her wrists, tied behind her back. The trap. That tie looked exactly like the trap at Destin's.

My wolf howled inside me, a cry of anguish that echoed through my bones. She wanted to run to them, to wrap herself around their legs and press her muzzle into their hands. She wanted to take Destin's pack to him, to guard him while he dressed.

Why were they here? Why did they look like this? I wanted to scream, to tear at the veil between us and pull them into my arms. But I couldn't move. My legs were leaden, my feet rooted to the ground.

YOU CAN SAVE HIM.

THIS WAS THE TEST, I was sure of it. I'd answered correctly with my brother, and now I was forced to look at another person I loved in trouble. Loved? The word pulsed through me. What we had wasn't love. It couldn't be. We'd known each other for a matter of days, and Destin . . . he was nothing like the mate I needed.

Alone. Living in shadows. I clenched my hands into fists. "What will happen to them?"

THAT IS NOT *for me to decide.*

OF COURSE it damn well wasn't. In the forest deep, a choice must be made. I wanted to save him. I wanted to save all of them. That voice said I had the power to do so. But where would it stop?

My lips trembled. I forced myself back, as far as I could go before the air snapped around me, forcing me to stay in that moment. "I will protect the pack," I whispered.

My wolf howled again, and it was a sound of pure agony. She wanted to leap through the mist, to tear down whatever barrier was keeping us apart. I wanted to join her, to let the rage and sorrow consume me.

And then, like a whisper on the wind, the voice. *Once an alpha used the power to save those he loved, only to see his pack crumble because of it . . .*

My breath hitched. This was the test. The ultimate challenge. To sacrifice my own desires. To wield the power of the Shadow Pack selflessly, or to succumb to the same fate as the alpha in the legend.

Destin was strong. My friends were strong. They could do this on their own, couldn't they?

My eyes dropped to the bone stalkers. To the three men.

I wanted to hold him. I wanted to feel his lips on my skin.

Love.

Tears streamed down my cheeks as I took a step back. "I'm sorry," I whispered, my voice breaking. "I'm so sorry."

TWENTY-TWO

Lana

For a moment, everything was still. Too still. There was nothing to distract from the ache growing in my chest. Then the light was back, but this time, it was brighter. More vibrant. It exploded from the woods around me, blinding me. I raised an arm to shield my face.

The light peaked, then slowly faded, but the realm didn't return to the muted hues of the misty woods. The view around me was clearer, crisper. I lowered my arm, squinting as my eyes adjusted to the new normal, and that's when I saw them.

Three figures stood in front of me, mere feet away. I blinked, trying to make sense of it. Were they part of the test? Had I passed?

I took a step back, my heart racing. They solidified, the light still too bright to make out details, but I could see that the one in the middle was holding something. *A book.* I swallowed hard, my mind racing. Were these the guardians of the relic? Or something else entirely? I had a million questions, but no words would come out.

They finally came into focus. They were warriors. The way they stood with their shoulders back. Their clothes. Worn leather armor covered their chests and shoulders, etched with intricate patterns.

"Daughter of the Shadow Pack, we're at your service." The warrior in the middle handed me the book.

My fingers trembled as I took it from him. "What is it?" I exhaled. "I mean, I know what it is, but what does it do? How does it work?"

He held my gaze. "It's a repository of power. Spells, rituals, and knowledge that the world has tried to forget. But the book doesn't just hold information—it has a will of its own."

I nodded, thinking of the dagger. I was getting used to that by now.

"It chooses who can read it. Those unworthy never see more than blank pages. The book tests the reader's mind—intellect, intent, and strength. And it doesn't give up its secrets without a price," he finished.

I let out a slow breath. So, I'd completed my tests, but the book still had to deem me worthy. "What kind of price?"

His expression hardened. "The more you draw from it, the more it draws from you. Every spell, every ritual, it takes a piece of your mind. The power to alter reality, predict the future, summon forces beyond comprehension—it's all in there." He paused, his lips pressed into a grim line. "But those who rely on it too much? They lose themselves."

THERE ONCE WAS *a man named Thorne* . . .

• • •

THE TWO OTHER warriors stepped forward. "We have been waiting."

"For what?"

"For you to claim your place."

Goosebumps rose on my skin. "And what place is that?"

The middle warrior stepped closer, placing his hand on the book I held. "You are the alpha of the Shadow Pack."

I blinked, trying to process his words. They seemed to hover at the surface, then sank into me with such force, I momentarily forgot to breathe. "I don't know—I don't have any experience with this."

He patted the book. "This is your guide. Your heritage. Everything you need to know is within these pages."

"If I'm worthy?"

The corner of his mouth lifted, then he stepped back between his shadow brothers. "What will you have us do?"

My thoughts were a tangled mess. What was I supposed to do with this new information? How was I supposed to lead a pack that I didn't even know existed until a week ago? And what about my friends? My family? What about everything I'd just seen in the vision?

I couldn't do this alone.

My heart ached, and my mind drifted to Destin. He was my anchor, the one constant in the midst of this chaos. I let my thoughts drift to the memory of him, his hands on my face, his lips on mine. The way he kissed me. Like he needed me. I wanted him here with me. Was that selfish?

I drew a deep breath, my chest tight. The air was cool and crisp, the leaves rustling softly in the breeze. The forest floor was soft beneath my feet. It was like the woods were breathing with me, their energy pulsing with my own.

"This feels heavy. This responsibility?" the middle warrior asked.

"You think?" I clutched the book to my chest.

"You now hold the weight of our pack, but you also have abilities. Gifts that come with your new role."

I frowned. "Abilities?"

The warrior on the left stepped forward. "You can move between shadow and light. Between this realm and the world you know."

I blinked. "What do you mean?"

He motioned to the shadows at the edge of the clearing. "Watch." He stepped into the darkness, and I gasped as he disappeared. My heart pounded, and I took a step forward, but the middle warrior held up a hand.

"Wait."

I stopped, my breath coming in shallow bursts. Then, as if nothing had happened, the warrior reappeared on the opposite side of the clearing.

I stared, my mind struggling to comprehend what I'd just seen. "How did he . . . ?"

"You have the same ability. You can move between worlds, Lana." The middle warrior's eyes twinkled with amusement.

I swallowed hard, a mix of awe and fear churning in my gut. "But I don't know how to do that."

The warrior smiled, his expression softening. "You will learn. We will help you."

I nodded, but my thoughts were already spiraling. If I could move between worlds, that meant I could go back. Back to the real world. Back to Destin.

I turned to the warriors. "Show me how."

TWENTY-THREE

DESTIN

The stone behind me lit up like a damn LED light, blinding in the darkening twilight. I didn't question it. As James turned, I took full advantage of the distraction and flew forward, my wolf taking over. Claws ripped from my fingers, my jaw cracked, and I tore out of my skin, fur bursting from my pores. I landed on all fours, then streaked forward like a missile.

I hip-checked Kael out of the way, then dove straight for the stalkers. Their claws were like needles tearing through my fur, and the stench of rot hit me like a brick wall. I went for their necks, but they were too fast. They jumped back, then lunged, snapping around my throat.

I tore at the one on my right, but the other one clamped down on my shoulder, tearing skin and muscle. I howled, then shoved the one on my left back, snapping my jaws over its head.

The two other alphas shifted next to me, diving into the fray, but I didn't have any help. Kael and the others were still bound. I fought with a wild ferocity, my claws tearing through fur and flesh. They slashed at me. My blood sprayed, they howled and thrashed as I lashed out.

Pain shot through my body as they bit back, their teeth sinking into my flank. I yanked free, tearing skin and muscle, then lunged again. My jaws clamped down on one of their necks, and I felt the satisfying crunch of bone. I shook my head, ripping it free, then threw the limp body to the side. I didn't know who it was, there was only the enemy.

The other stalker lunged for my throat, but I was ready. I thrashed, pulling it off balance, then slammed it into the ground. I didn't give it a chance to recover. I tore into its flesh, ripping it apart until it was nothing but a pile of gore and bone.

It would regenerate, but I hoped it would give me a little time. I turned, ready to face the other stalker, but one of the alphas was already on me. His claws sank into my back, and I howled in pain. I twisted, trying to shake him off, but he held on. I drove my body backward, slamming him against a tree. The impact knocked the wind out of me, but it also forced the alpha to release his grip.

I spun, my vision red, my breath wheezing. My fur was slick with blood, my legs unsteady, but I didn't care. I would protect them. I was—

"Enough!" James' voice cut through the night like a knife. The bone stalkers froze, their eyes locking onto him. The other alphas, who had been shifting and growling at the edge of the clearing, dropped their heads. Their shoulders hunched, just as a weight landed on my back. *What the hell?*

"Stop," James said again, his voice soft as the weight crushed me, forcing me down on my front paws.

Then a figure stepped out of the shadows. My wolf whined, urging me forward, but I couldn't move. I could barely lift my eyes to see that it was her. Lana. The book clutched in her arms.

The glow from the stone bathed her in light, making her appear almost ethereal. No, not ethereal. She was there. Solid. More vivid than the shadows that fell around her. Like she was in hyper focus while the rest of the world blurred around her.

My muscles twitched to life. I pushed against the weight of James's power, my frustration growing as I realized I couldn't push past it. I couldn't shift. Couldn't even think straight.

Lana's eyes found mine, and her lips parted. She turned on James, her expression hardening. "Why?"

James took a step toward her, but Lana didn't flinch. "I'm so glad you joined us."

She held her ground, her grip tightening on the book. Her eyes glowed with a fierce determination, and for a moment, I thought I saw something else flicker there. I growled, working to give her a signal, to bark, yip, anything to tell her to run. This power James had, I'd never felt anything like it.

Lana ignored his smug comment. "Why did you bring them here?" She motioned to the bone stalkers. The creatures growled low in their throats, but James held up a hand, and they fell silent.

"They answer to me," James said simply.

Lana shook her head. "They answer to no one."

James raised an eyebrow. "And how would you know that?" Lana's wolf pulsed through her, the veins in her neck standing out, but James only laughed. "I see, because you've glimpsed something beyond this world, you think you understand the darkness? Because you hold that book—"

Lana hissed as he reached forward. "Don't."

His smile widened. "But you see, that and the dagger you hold will answer to me, too. You were wonderfully willing to retrieve it for me, but now I can remove that burden." He held out his hands like an expectant father.

Lana stood perfectly still, her eyes searing into his. "Please. Take it."

James sneered at Lana, then lunged forward. His eyes flashed with a feral intensity, and his silhouette stretched and contorted as he reached for the book. *No.* I panted, fighting the weight that locked me to the ground. He seemed to be one with the shadows, ready to rip into her and—

Three streaks of gold shot from the stone. The lights blazed across the clearing, and I felt their brilliance before I saw them. They were like shooting stars, fast and furious, and in the blink of an eye, they hammered into Evelyn, Rowan, Callista, and Kael.

Evelyn staggered, her eyes widening. Rowan cursed, and Kael stumbled back with Callista, his head snapping to the side as if he'd been physically struck. Then, just as quickly as they'd been hit, the three of them straightened. They were free. Their bands removed.

The streaks of light ignited everything in their path with a searing brilliance. The bone stalkers, looming with their skeletal frames and empty, glowing eyes, shrieked in unison. Their twisted bodies convulsed as flames licked up their limbs, burning brighter and hotter with every second. The shrikes tore from the trees, but not fast enough.

The scent of charred bone filled the air, thick and acrid, clawing at the back of my throat. The stalkers' limbs spasmed, twisting at impossible angles as they writhed in agony, but the flames showed no mercy. They were consumed, their forms crumbling into ash that scattered across the clearing like dark snowflakes. Feathers rained from the sky.

I sucked in a breath, forcing myself upright, my muscles trembling from the effort. The weight that had held me down moments before was gone. My gaze snapped to Lana just as James snarled, his hand still outstretched toward the book. The flames closed in, gold threads twisting through the air like snakes ready to strike. Realization flickered across his face—he was trapped. They were all trapped.

Then, the air shifted.

A dense, choking plume of smoke exploded from James's chest, billowing outward and swallowing the alphas whole. It was as if reality itself twisted around them, bending space and light, sucking them into a vortex of darkness. The smoke coiled like a living thing, thick and suffocating, and the clearing plunged into a deafening silence as the alphas vanished.

One second they were there, faces twisted in rage—and the next, gone. Lana took a shaky step forward, her gaze locked on the spot where James had disappeared.

Kael cursed under his breath, fists clenched at his sides as he let out a strangled cry into the trees. Rowan stood next to him, his face a mask of fury. I understood exactly. The alphas needed to pay, but right then, all I cared about was her.

The streaks of gold solidified, shifting from abstract streaks to defined shapes. They grew taller, more substantial. What had been mere lines of light turned into fur and muscle, their forms expanding until they stood as wolves in the middle of the clearing.

I would've marveled more if Lana hadn't raced forward. She bolted toward me, her eyes locked on mine. I lunged, meeting her halfway, and Lana didn't slow. She crashed into me, her arms wrapping around my neck, her head burying into my blood-soaked fur.

Every fiber of my being screamed to hold her, to shift back and pull her into my arms, but I was still weak, my body healing. Lana's breath hitched, the vibration of a sob emanating from her chest.

I growled, forcing my human form forward despite the pain. My fur retracted, my bones reshaped. As I stood there, naked in the clearing, I didn't give a single shit about the others seeing me like this.

I pulled her into my arms, my hands gripping her shoulders, her back, her hair. She looked up at me, her eyes glassy with tears. "Lana—" I pulled her tighter, feeling her heartbeat against my chest. When her lips finally met mine, it was like the world stopped. The chaos of the battle, the confusion, the fear, all of it faded into the background.

Her breath was warm, her lips soft, and I lost myself in her. I wanted to claim her right then and there in the dirt, but the sound of a throat clearing snapped me back to reality. I pulled back, my eyes meeting Lana's. She was flushed, her eyes glassy, and I couldn't help but smile at the sight. Then I remembered we were standing in the middle of a clearing, and I was buck-naked.

Lana's cheeks turned a deeper shade of pink as she glanced down between us. She quickly turned, grabbing my pack and handing it to me. I pulled out my clothes and dressed quickly, my eyes constantly flicking back to Lana. She was different. More solid, more . . . I didn't know how to describe it.

I pulled on my shirt and turned, shoving my feet into my boots.

"Okay, what in the actual hell just happened?" Rowan finally broke the silence, his voice strained.

Callista stepped forward, her eyes wide. "Who are they?" She pointed at the three wolves still standing at attention behind Lana.

Kael paced, his hand running through his hair. "We need to go after them. The alphas. We can't just let them go."

Lana nodded. "We will. I promise." She stood and motioned to the warriors, her eyes flicking back to Rowan, then to me. "This is . . . my pack." I stilled, looking between her and the wolves. "I'm Shadow Pack, I—"

The wolves shifted to their human forms in a blink. One of them stepped forward. "She's our alpha."

Alpha. That was what I felt from her. I bristled, and my wolf, he didn't know what to think. We hated alphas. But Lana . . .

Lana locked eyes with me and swallowed hard. "I don't know what this means." She motioned at the book in her hands. "They say I'll learn, but—" Her eyes glistened with tears. "I don't know how to do this."

It felt like that power had landed back on my shoulders. "Do what?"

Her face broke. "Say goodbye."

The shifter warriors stepped forward. They were tall, imposing figures, their eyes sharp and their movements precise. One of them, a man with dark hair and piercing eyes, spoke first. "You are Shadow Pack now, Lana. You must start by finding Shadow Pack blood."

Lana glanced down at the dagger on her hip. "How?"

My pulse quickened. I knew that look. She'd gotten it in the maze and on the crumbling stone steps. Then as she'd conjured flames and launched them at a bone stalker. "Lana—"

The warrior spoke. "You are alpha. You will know."

Lana lifted her head, her wolf pressing toward me so intently, her eyes glowed. My wolf stood at attention, as if readying to answer her call. "Lana." My voice was low and rough. I didn't know what I was saying. What she was trying to say to me.

She stepped forward, lifting the dagger from its hilt.

TWENTY-FOUR

Lana

I couldn't do this. Not by myself. It wasn't selfishness, it wasn't using my newfound power to get what I wanted. I had been tasked with building a pack, with hunting down the other relics, and the only way I'd found the book was with Destin's help.

All my life I'd believed alphas were the strength of the pack, but I'd had it all wrong. The pack was the strength of the alpha.

"Lana, what are you doing." Destin's breath came quickly. I would make this fast.

"You don't want a pack. You don't want an alpha, I know this. But you have a Shadow Pack heart." Destin frowned. He opened his mouth, but I placed a finger over his lips. "You didn't want to take me to the stone, but you did."

"You forced me—"

I pressed harder against his mouth. "You stayed in the shadow realm, you were the reason I completed the challenges, and we were still able to help your wolves."

The three warriors stepped forward. Their eyes, sharp and discerning, scanned over Destin. "He's not Shadow Pack," the tallest warrior stated, his voice deep and authoritative.

I dropped my finger. "You don't know that."

The second warrior crossed his arms over his chest. "We can sense it. His blood doesn't carry the mark."

My voice trembled with intensity. "And yet I've seen him. I know his heart." I held up a hand to silence them from another retort, never breaking my gaze with his. "Where I'm going, you can't follow unless you're Shadow Pack."

My wolf pressed against my consciousness, the pressure so intense, I blinked to clear my vision.

I lifted a hand to Destin's jaw. "Would you follow me? Would you let me be your pack?"

His fists clenched, and he pressed his lips together. His jaw tightened, the muscles in his neck straining. "I can't leave my wolves."

I nodded. "I know. They're your family." I took another step closer, my heart pounding in my chest. "But if you could. If you could have both. Your wolves and me, would you?" I swallowed hard. "Would you let me be your alpha? Your mate?"

There was a flicker of something in his eyes. A glimmer of hope, or maybe it was desperation. The same desperation I felt. I couldn't do this by myself.

I dropped my hand to his chest, then closed my eyes and tried to feel. To sense the energy flowing through him, just like he'd shown me. It was like standing on the edge of a river, the current rushing past, just out of my reach. I needed to step in, to let the water flow over my skin. I took a deep breath and imagined myself wading into that river, feeling the icy cold seep into my bones.

Then it was there. All of it. His pain, his fear. I was plunged into the storm. I didn't know exactly what I was trying to do, but I listened. Floated. I thought of the river flowing through me, and I pictured it merging with his. Like two tributaries coming together to form a single, more powerful current.

"Lana, what are you doing?" Destin gasped.

I took a deep breath and tried to speak, but the words wouldn't come. I was too *full.*

His breath was ragged, and I could feel his heartbeat under my palm. "You don't want to see that part of me. It's not—"

I pushed harder, and his eyes widened. He was afraid. Not of me, but of what I would find. Of the darkness lurking beneath the surface. His wild, untamed parts that I already loved.

The rivers linked, and while I knew he could feel me, I flooded every piece of my own emotions into him. The way my heart ached every time I saw him, the way my skin tingled when he touched me. The way I needed him more than air.

I felt his resistance, the walls he'd built around himself, and my wolf surged through me, searching, longing for his. *You don't have to be alone. Neither of us have to do this alone.*

"Yes." Destin panted, gripping my hand with his. "Yes, Lana. I would be your mate."

My eyes flew open, and before I understood what I was doing, I lifted the dagger and turned Destin's hand in mine.

"Lana, wait!" Callista stepped forward, her eyes wide.

My eyes snapped to hers, and Callie startled. I don't know what she saw there, but the blood drained from her face. "Trust me, Callie."

She nodded once and stepped back. I dropped the blade to my hand, and it cut easily through my skin, releasing a crimson stream that coated the metal. Destin hissed as I did the same over his palm.

Instantly, the dagger vibrated, surging forward like it had at the pools the first time I'd let it taste my blood. I wrenched my arm back, then turned my hand and slammed my bloody palm against his.

TWENTY-FIVE

DESTIN

Heat seared through me the moment our palms pressed together, Lana's blood mixing with mine. It was more than pain—it was energy, raw and unfiltered, surging through every nerve like wildfire. The connection between us locked tight, and I couldn't pull away even if I wanted to. Her pulse slammed into mine, relentless, merging until I couldn't tell where her heartbeat ended and mine began.

My wolf surged forward, wild and howling, claws raking at the inside of my skin. The bond wasn't gentle—it was furious and consuming, burning through all my defenses. My muscles strained as the force pressed down on us both, and for one brief moment, it felt as if I'd unravel, as if everything I'd built inside myself—walls, anger, solitude—would collapse.

And then, just as violently as it came, the pressure released. My hand ripped away from hers, and I dropped to my knees, gasping. Beside me, Lana knelt too, her breath ragged. Blood smeared across both our palms, bright and vivid. Something in the air shifted. I was a lone wolf. I didn't do connections. I didn't do bonds or packs or any of that bullshit. But this? This was something different. Something I couldn't deny even if I wanted to.

Kael surged forward, and Lana was on her feet in an instant, lunging to block his advance. "Don't take another step closer to my mate."

Mate. I stared at my palm, the wound she'd cut with the dagger already sealing closed, and in its place, the head of a wolf in half shadow, half light. Lana had marked me, but not with teeth or claws. *With her blood.*

Kael held up his hand and stepped back. Behind him, the three warriors had shifted into their wolf forms. They prowled closer, and then, in a smooth, fluid motion, Lana shifted.

Her wolf exploded forward—larger, more regal than I remembered. Her fur was still gray and white, but now it gleamed with a new power, her shoulders broader, her frame taller. A leather satchel appeared around her neck, the dagger and book suddenly gone from the ground, tucked next to her heart.

She stood at full height, looking more like an alpha than any wolf I'd ever seen. My wolf stirred at the sight of her, wild admiration rippling through me. She was stunning—strong, commanding, untouchable.

Not for me, she wasn't. *Mate.* Heat coiled low in my gut, spreading like a fever through my limbs. My hands curled into fists, nails biting into my palms. My skin felt too tight. Lana had marked me, but my wolf stirred violently, and every fiber of control I'd gained around Lana snapped like a twig.

"Lana." My voice was rough. Desperate. I wanted that bed in the forest. I wanted to take her there against the rock wall and prove that I was worthy of her. That I had the strength to live up to the glorious creature in front of me.

And then I heard her. Not her voice in the air, but in my mind. *My blood is your blood.* The words hit me like brick wall, the bond between us roaring alive. Her presence wasn't just near—it was *inside* me, woven into every cell in my body.

"Lana," I pleaded, my hands already trembling. I needed her, or I was going to crumble. Shatter. Burst at the seams.

Lana's eyes were dark as she turned to the warriors, daring any of them to challenge her. *I have claimed a mate,* she announced. *I thought being strong meant figuring out how to do this alone. But my strength isn't in solitude. My strength is in my pack.*

Her eyes locked on to each of theirs in turn, and she held her head higher. *I am your alpha, and though I will be in the shadow realm, I need both of my packs to find the remaining relics. I will come for you.*

One of the warriors stepped forward, his head lowered. *You can't stay here forever.*

Lana dipped her head. *I understand.* She turned back to the others. *I am a part of both packs. A protector to both. Of all.*

Lana's head swiveled back to Kael. *The alphas don't have the book. They've seen this display of power and will most likely lay low for a time.*

He'd asked her a question. She was speaking to them through the pack bond. She was speaking to me. Emotion washed over me when I realized it had been over ten years since I'd heard another wolf in my head. Over twenty since I'd welcomed it.

Kael clenched his jaw. "Then we'll find the alphas before they come out of hiding."

No, you won't. Lana's voice was a growl. She turned to Kael, Callista, Evelyn, and Rowan, her eyes softening. *Go back,* she told them, her voice quieter now but no less commanding. *I'll come to you when we figure out our next move.*

I gritted my teeth. I didn't care about the damn alphas. I knew I should have, that the safety of my wolves depended on it, but all I could see was her.

Lana finally turned to me. Her golden eyes locked onto mine, and the weight of her gaze rooted me in place. *Will you come with me?*

The question hit me harder than I expected. Her words weren't a command—they were an invitation. Being claimed by her didn't feel like losing myself. It felt like waking up for the first time in years. Without a word, I stepped forward and reached out, running my hand through the thick fur along her neck. Her warmth seeped into me, the bond between us thrumming with quiet power.

I never wanted to be owned, and I sure as hell never wanted to own anyone else. But this . . . this was belonging.

Lana walked forward, and the fabric of the world rippled around us. I didn't hesitate. I shifted into my wolf form and moved with her, the two of us stepping into the shadows as one.

CHAPTER
TWENTY-SIX

Lana

The shadow realm swirled around us, an ephemeral haze that blurred the edges of reality. Destin's wolf was a dark silhouette beside me, his eyes gleaming with an otherworldly light. My own paws moved soundlessly over the indistinct ground, each step sending ripples through the misty landscape.

I wasn't sure who was leading, but when we ended up in front of Destin's cabin, I decided it was me. From the moment I'd seen Destin in his room stripping off his shirt, I knew I wasn't done with this place. Even if I hadn't been able to see this far at the time.

I stopped, remembering the emotions I'd felt in him back at Lava Forks. I closed my eyes and thought of what we needed, then opened them to find it in front of us.

"How did—?" Destin strode forward to the sandwiches that appeared on a low table standing in the hibernating grass.

"You were hungry."

Destin grunted and dug in. I joined him, both of us eating our fill. When we finished, the table faded back into the mist.

This time, there was no struggle to push through the gauzy film. I didn't have to slash the world with my dagger. We simply moved into the real world like passing through a door. The cabin materialized around us. The wooden beams and rustic decor solidified, and suddenly, we were standing in Destin's bedroom in our human forms, our clothing forgotten in the mountains.

I dropped the satchel at the foot of his bed. All this time, I'd thought my journey was to find the relics, that the power I was seeking was within them. I had yet to discover what they meant for me—what they meant for all of us—but I couldn't think about that at the moment.

My wolf and every cell in my body was focused on the man in front of me. If the universe brought me a mate, it damn well better understand that I needed a minute to enjoy him.

Destin's eyes locked on mine, and for a moment, we only stared. His chest rose and fell with each breath, the muscles rippling under his skin. He was beautiful. *He was mine.*

Destin moved forward and took me into his arms. I gasped at the intensity of his hands on my hips, his fingers pulling me tighter to him. "You made me wait," he murmured, his lips traveling over my jaw, my neck.

"I had to take care of—" I sucked in a breath as Destin sucked my earlobe into his mouth.

"How did you know it would work?" His voice whispered against my cheek. I opened my eyes and met his.

"I don't know," I admitted, my voice breathless. "But I couldn't live without you."

Destin growled low in his throat and pressed his forehead to mine. His hand moved to the back of my neck, his thumb stroking my skin. "If you're searching for the relics, how will I protect these wolves?"

I exhaled slowly. "I can move through the shadow realm. I'll never have to be gone long."

Destin scoffed. "If you think you're leaving without me, you're crazy." He tugged, leading me to his bed. "Not as impressive as the one in the woods, but it serves its purpose."

I dropped to my back over his quilt, pulling him with me. "It smells like you. That's all I want." I needed his scent. I wanted him to cover every inch of me with it. Hilarious that only a few days ago I was trying to wash it off.

He smirked, but all traces of amusement disappeared as he leaned in and crushed his lips against mine. He was all tongue and teeth, rough and desperate. His hands wrapped around me like he was drowning and I was his buoy. His fingers left an impression.

"I can't be gentle," he gasped. "I need you Lana. If I don't claim you, I'm going to die."

I sighed, my body arching into him. "Claim me, Destin. Please."

He pulled my legs higher, throwing them over his shoulders and pressing his weight against me. His hands wrapped around my thighs, dragging me flush against him. I cried out in pleasure, my hands tangling in his quilt. "Destin—"

"Out there you're an alpha. Out there you have to be strong. But in here?" His breaths were ragged as he toyed with me. He moved tantalizingly slowly, every tremble and whimper from my body only egging him on. "In here, you can let go, Lana."

Every nerve in my body was a live wire, my blood pounding in my ears. It was like a wave crashing over me, pulling me under and then throwing me to the surface. I grasped onto his forearms, letting him anchor me.

"You belong with me," he growled as his body heaved, his fingers digging into my skin so hard, they would leave marks.

With. Not *to*. Destin had never wanted a wolf to own, he'd made that crystal clear. And even though I was the Shadow Pack alpha, he didn't bow to me.

We were equals. My blood was his blood. Our paths were bound, our fates fused.

"Right here," I whispered. "Only you."

"*My mate.*"

I couldn't hold on. I didn't want to. I released my hold on the physical world as he drove me higher, letting the wave take me. My nails bit into his arms, and as I crashed over the edge, Destin turned his head, his teeth breaking the skin of my inner thigh.

I gasped, euphoria pulsing through me, white light bursting behind my eyes.

He was marking me. Claiming me. And I wanted nothing more than to let him.

I LAY ON MY SIDE, my head on Destin's chest. The morning sun filtered through the curtains. Birds chirped outside the cabin, their songs a gentle reminder that the world continued to turn, even when everything in my life had flipped on its head.

Destin's arm was draped over my waist, his fingers tracing lazy circles on my skin. I rolled to my back, the bed creaking beneath us, and his grip tightened. "Where do you think you're going?" His voice was thick with sleep.

I smiled, turning back and nuzzling into him. "Nowhere."

He grunted in approval, his hand sliding lower. I shivered as his fingers brushed against my inner thigh, over the new mark I bore there.

"We should get cleaned up."

He groaned, but I was already sitting, pulling him with me. I stumbled, my legs still wobbly from the night before, and he caught me with a smirk.

I followed him toward the bathroom, glancing down at the leather satchel still sitting on the floor. I would look at the book. Eventually. *But would I be ready to know the things it wanted to share?*

I met Destin in the bathroom, a small room with a basin sink and a shower head mounted above it. Destin moved to the hand pump, and I watched as he started to pump water.

I balked. "Is that going to be cold?"

He shot me a look. "I'm not a neanderthal. I have a solar heater."

I gave him a playful shove, and he grinned, then turned back to the pump. Water splashed into the basin, and he tested it with his hand. "There you go. Hot enough for you, princess?"

I blushed, then butterflied my leg out in front of the mirror to look at it again. Destin's mark. A delicate crown etched into my skin.

Destin slipped his hand over my hip and down my skin until his fingers traced the lines.

I lay my head back against his shoulder. "It's perfect."

He pushed against my hip, flipping me around so our bodies were flush. "You're perfect."

I closed my eyes, wrapping my arms around him, pressing my cheek against his chest. I had reading to do, but it could wait a few more moments.

If I thought too far into the future, fear paralyzed me. From the moment I'd used the dagger, every path I'd envisioned for myself splintered, fractured, or disappeared completely. I was taking step after step into the dark, trusting my instincts and the few things I knew.

I'd always been good at taking orders, but had no experience giving them. I was strong, but in Destin's arms, I had permission to be fragile.

I could walk into the unknown with him by my side.

After breathing him in for a solid minute, I opened my eyes and pulled back. I pressed my lips to his jaw, then frowned as something caught my eye out the window behind him.

"What is it?" Destin turned, his gaze following mine. He tensed. "What the hell?"

"That's not normal, right?" I already knew the answer. The smoke was too dark, too thick. It was coming from a spot deeper in the forest, far from any of the cabins I'd seen on our way in.

He shook his head, his jaw clenched.

My mind flew back to when we stood outside the she-wolf's hut. "I conjured fire," I whispered. "Did we check that it was put out?" Panic gripped my heart.

Destin grabbed my hand and pulled me back into the bedroom. "I don't know. But we're going to have to find a way to stop it."

EPILOGUE

MIA

I shoved open the door to the mechanic shop, and the bell above the door frame clanged as the door swung back shut. The smell of grease and rubber filled my nose, and the hum of machinery buzzed from the back of the shop. I scanned the room, searching for someone—anyone—who could help.

My eyes landed on Tori sitting behind the desk, her fingers flying over a keyboard. I rushed over, my breath coming in ragged gasps as I skidded to a stop in front of her. Tori looked up, her eyes widening in surprise. "Mia?" She pushed her chair back, standing. "What's wrong?"

I opened my mouth, but all that came out was a wheezy exhale. I took a moment to catch my breath, then blurted, "I just saw the news. There's a fire. Up north. Where Rowan and the others are."

Tori's eyes narrowed. "What kind of fire?"

I shook my head. "They didn't say much, just that it was in

the middle of nowhere. Not near any serviceable roads. And that the fire stations up there are few and far between."

Tori frowned and grabbed the remote on the desk, turning on the television hanging over their waiting area. The news flickered on, and she flipped through the channels until she found one with a banner running along the bottom of the screen.

FIRE BREAKS Out Near Secluded Home in Northern British Columbia

MY HEART POUNDED as the news anchor spoke, describing the scene. "A fire has broken out in a remote area of Northern British Columbia, posing challenges for emergency responders due to its location far from main roads. The blaze started near a solitary, rustic home in the woods, and with limited fire stations in the region, containment efforts are expected to be slow."

Tori's knuckles turned white as she gripped the edge of the desk. "They're smart. There's nothing we can do, but I'm sure—"

"There's nothing you can do?" I hissed. "There are packs up there. Can't you send them to help?"

She gritted her teeth. "My people are already tracking a threat, and Jasper is dealing with a situation with a newly pregnant she-wolf. We're stretched thin, Mia." Tori blew out a breath. "And you know the northern packs. They don't want to help. They don't want to get involved."

I clenched my fists. "I've heard about their alphas."

Tori's eyes flashed. "It's not our job to—"

"The northern alphas only care about themselves. You know that!" I shook my head.

Tori's eyes narrowed. "Why do you care so much, Mia?"

It was a fair question. Besides loving our forests, I'd given her no reason to take my concern seriously. My throat tightened, and I blinked to stop the tears from coming. "My sister is a rogue."

Tori's eyebrows lifted. "Your sister?"

I nodded, my vision blurring. "The last I heard from her, she was living up north. In the mountains." I swallowed hard. "I know her. She won't leave if there are people in danger."

Tori's lips parted, and she paused for a long moment before finally saying, "Mia—"

"I have to find her." I shoved my hands in my pockets, my lips pulling into a tight line.

Tori nodded, then met my eyes. "You shouldn't go alone."

I BURST out of the mechanic shop and sprinted to my car. My heart pounded in my chest, adrenaline pushing me. My hands shook as I fumbled with my keys, finally managing to unlock the door and slide into the driver's seat.

I started the engine and pulled out onto the street, barely glancing at the speed limit signs as I sped toward home. The world outside blurred, a mix of green trees and gray pavement.

I slammed on the brakes in front of my apartment building and ran inside. My mind raced as I grabbed a backpack from my closet and started shoving essentials into it. Clothes, a flashlight, a first aid kit. I paused, then added a map of the area. I didn't know if I'd need it, but something told me it would be useful.

I took a deep breath, trying to steady my racing thoughts.

You shouldn't go alone. I needed help. Someone who knew the area, someone who would be willing to drop everything and come with me.

Liam.

I swung the backpack over my shoulder and rushed out of the apartment, not bothering to lock the door behind me. I jumped into the car and tore down the street to his place.

I parked and ran up the front steps, my breath coming in ragged gasps. I pounded on the door, barely giving it a second before I knocked again.

Liam answered, his hair tousled and eyes bleary. "Mia? What the hell—"

"There's a fire," I said, cutting him off. "Up north. Where Rowan and Evelyn are. I just saw it on the news. Tori says there isn't anything they can do about it because the northern packs are supposed to handle it, but we both know they won't—"

Liam held up a hand. "Whoa, whoa. Start over?"

I took a shuddering breath. "There's a fire. In the mountains. I think my sister is up there."

Liam blinked, then rubbed a hand over his face. "Seriously?"

I nodded, my heart still pounding in my chest. "I need to find her. I need to make sure she's okay."

Liam didn't hesitate. "Give me a minute." He disappeared into the house, and I heard him rummaging around. A minute later, he reappeared with a backpack slung over his shoulder. "Okay, let's go."

We got in the car, and I sped down Main, my hands tight on the wheel, my thoughts racing as fast as the tires on the pavement. When we passed through town, I couldn't believe what I was seeing. It was like a scene out of a movie. Firemen in reflective gear, hoses and tools being organized, fire trucks and volunteers packing their vehicles with supplies. The smell of smoke hung in the air, making my eyes water.

I slammed on the brakes and screeched to the curb.

"Mia!" Liam complained, but I jumped out of the car and ran up to one of the firemen.

"What's going on?" I asked.

He glanced at me, then continued strapping a hose to the side of a truck. "We've got a hot spot crew heading north. Volunteers are going with them to help with containment."

I nodded, trying to process the information. "That fire in the mountains? The one on the news?"

"Yeah," he said gruffly. "It's bad. No stations out there to respond, so we're all hands on deck."

I swallowed hard. "Thank you." I turned and jogged back to the car, my mind already working out what needed to happen next.

Liam eyed me as I climbed in behind the wheel. "What'd he say?"

"They're organizing a crew to head north. Looks like they're already packing up." I put the car in drive, then pulled up the street a little ways and parked.

Liam frowned. "So, what do you want to do? Follow them, or—"

I shook my head and reached into the back seat. "If we want to get close, we're going to have to go with them." I knew my sister. She wasn't living somewhere with easy access from the main roads, and my guess was that everything up there was going to be blocked off.

Liam's eyes widened. "What? Mia, we can't just—"

I grabbed my jacket and backpack, then stepped out of the car. "We have to get up there, Liam. My sister—"

"You don't even know if—"

"Stop," I snapped, my frustration boiling over. "We can't

wait and hope the northern packs do something. We both know they won't. They have no reason to."

Liam exhaled slowly, his breath visible in the cold air. "Okay. But we're not firemen. We don't have the training. We don't have the right gear."

I pulled the straps of my backpack tighter. That was exactly why we needed to go with them. "It's just a ride, Liam."

He stared at me for a long moment, then sighed. "Alright." He turned and started toward the fire station, his shoulders tense. "But if we die, I'm blaming you."

BUY BOOK #4 IN THE SERIES

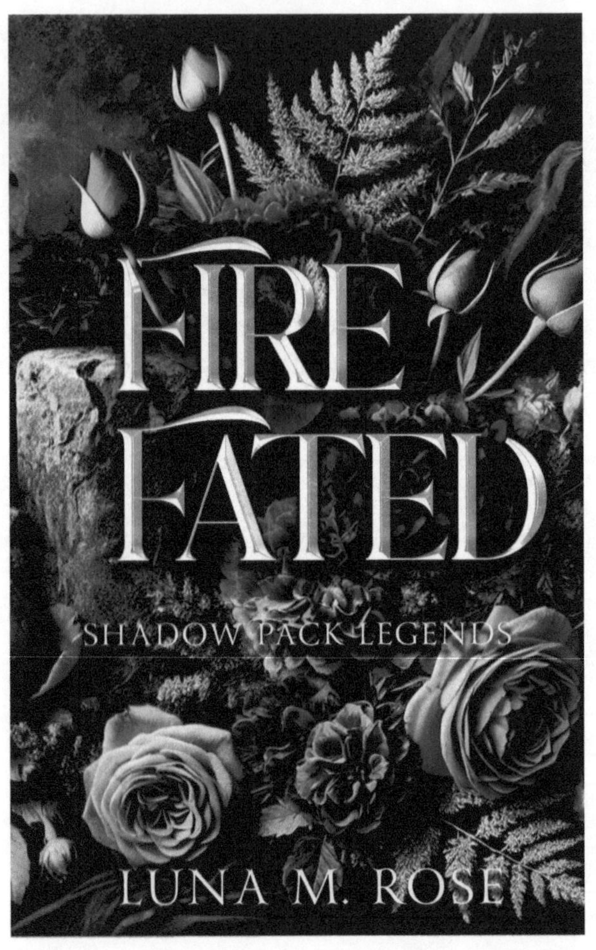
FIRE
FATED
SHADOW PACK LEGENDS
LUNA M. ROSE

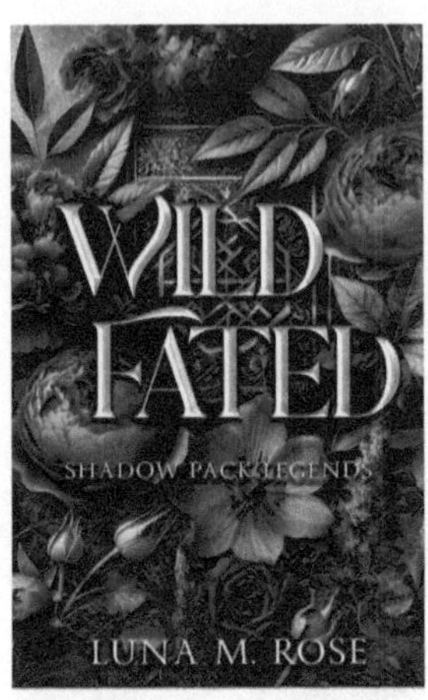

WILD
FATED
SHADOW PACK LEGENDS
LUNA M. ROSE

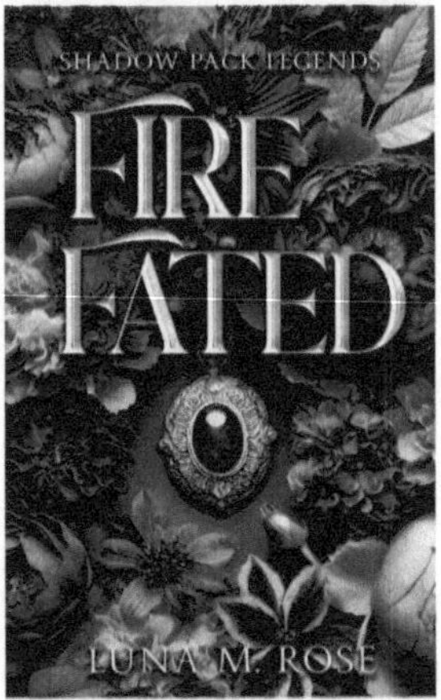

SHADOW PACK LEGENDS
FIRE
FATED
LUNA M. ROSE

BLOOD
FATED
SHADOW PACK LEGENDS
LUNA M. ROSE

I WON'T
DATE
THE
WOLF
PRINCE
WOLF ISLAND SEASON 1
LUNA M. ROSE

About the Author

 Luna masquerades as a well-adjusted, functioning adult, but she secretly still believes in magic and wild things hidden just beyond the veil of our world. She has a fairy garden (with lights!) and lives with her husband and children near the Rocky Mountains in Colorado. She adores shiny objects.

9 781955 286688